The Topless Widow
of Herkimer Street

The Topless Widow
of Herkimer Street

Stories

JACOB M. APPEL

HOWLING BIRD PRESS

MINNEAPOLIS

2016

☙

HOWLING BIRD PRESS
MFA in Creative Writing
Augsburg College
2211 Riverside Avenue
Minneapolis, Minnesota 55454
www.augsburg.edu/mfa

Associate Editors: Katherine Berger, Patricia Fox, Cynthia Truitt Lynch
Book design: John Gaterud
Cover photograph: Krivosheev Vitaly
Text: Adobe Garamond Pro
Printed at Bookmobile, Minneapolis
First printing

☙

The stories collected in this book have previously appeared, sometimes in different form, in the following publications:
"The Current Occupant," *Beloit Fiction Journal*
"The Topless Widow of Herkimer Street," *Berkeley Fiction Review*
"Lessons in Platygaeanism," *Natural Bridge*
"Bioethics for Dunces," *The Seattle Review*
"The Wish," *North Dakota Quarterly*
"Toward Uncharted Waters," *Florida Review*
"Rendezvous in Wikiternity," *The Saranac Review*
"Long Term," *Prairie Schooner*

For Rosie, Ruth & Theia

❧

BOOKS BY JACOB M. APPEL

The Man Who Wouldn't Stand Up

Wedding Wipeout

The Biology of Luck

Scouting for the Reaper

Phoning Home

Einstein's Beach House

Miracles and Conundrums of the Secondary Planet

The Magic Laundry

Coulrophobia and Fata Morgana

THE TOPLESS WIDOW OF HERKIMER STREET: STORIES

The Current Occupant

IDIOT THAT HE WAS—and every time Lewinter dozed off, his wife woke him to remind him of his infernal stupidity—he'd bought a house from a mail-order catalog. An *online* catalog, but still! "Who buys a house from a catalog?" Isabelle griped. "What *century* do you live in?"

They'd checked into the nearest vacant motel, a tumbledown motor lodge twenty minutes over the New Hampshire line. Their room smelled vaguely of wet dog and disinfectant. Behind the headboard, the plumbing yowled and keened. The mattress felt like one colossal iron spring. Even if Isabelle hadn't poked his shoulder every thirty seconds, he'd have tossed fitfully until daybreak. What a difference twenty-four hours made! On Friday night, they'd been driving up from the city, greased in cheer, anticipating their first peek at the summer refuge for their golden years. They'd stayed at a bed & breakfast whose cornmeal scones earned superlatives as far south as West 96th Street. And nary a word of complaint from Isabelle about his means of procuring the house. She'd been just as pleased as he'd been for the discount, and the expediency, of a ready-made dwelling. Who needed the carpenter ants and stress that came with renovated farmsteads? But that was before she'd eyed the level concrete slab where their prefabricated paradise was to have been deposited three weeks earlier, before he'd phoned the manufacturer and asked a question equally slapstick and infuriating: How in heaven's name can you deliver a *house* to the wrong address?

"Are you *sure* you gave them the correct location?" Isabelle asked.

She'd gone off her antidepressant only weeks before, a perennial source of conflict. With the Cymbalta, she couldn't pee; drug-free, she ranted over minutiae.

"Yes, I'm sure. It's their mistake."

But Lewinter was only 99.9 percent sure, not 100 percent. He'd filled in the location over the Internet alongside his bank's SWIFT code. Who could say he hadn't plugged in the wrong town or acceded to the wrong auto-correction? Not that it mattered. The bottom line was that they'd have to locate the structure in Hager's Corners themselves, and then hire a transport outfit on their own dime to haul it back to Hager's Notch, to the twenty-eight lakefront acres they'd inherited years earlier from Isabelle's bachelor uncle. After a decade of shelling out taxes for the unused parcel, the moment had finally come to milk some pleasure from the property.

"What if we can't find it?" Isabelle pressed. "Or what if they just abandoned it by the side of the highway and it's become a hangout for crystal-meth addicts?"

"In three whole weeks?" Lewinter asked. He stumbled out of bed and groped his way into the bathroom, leaving the door ajar as he urinated.

"The Hindenburg burned in fifteen seconds," Isabelle called.

Before their oldest daughter was born, she'd taught high-school history for two years, which rendered her a self-styled expert.

"I'll keep that in mind," said Lewinter, retracing his steps, "if I ever buy a Zeppelin."

"All I'm saying is a lot can happen in three weeks."

He kissed the exposed flesh above her collarbone. How familiar she was—her body, her henna bangs, the contours of her cynicism. How familiar, and for all her carping, how comforting. After thirty-seven years of marriage and three children, he knew exactly what came next: "Half a million men died in *one* week during the Battle of the Marne…."

"And the Nazis flattened Rotterdam in three hours," Lewinter rejoined. "I know all about it. Now let's get some sleep."

☙

AT DAYBREAK THE NEXT MORNING, they checked out of the motel and set off for the tiny blemish on the map that was Hager's Corners. Lewinter had arranged coverage for his patients only through Sunday, and he was scheduled to extract cataracts starting at 7 o'clock Monday morning, so he wanted the house-locating and schlepping finished quickly. In his fantasies, they tracked down the dwelling and arrived back in Manhattan early enough for a twilight jog around Central Park. His goal was to shed another fifteen pounds by Memorial Day. "So I can fit into my bikini," he quipped to their Armenian doorman, but his real fear was the leaden arteries that had felled so many of his contemporaries at the hospital. He'd turned sixty-four that February, the same age that his own father had died, and every twinge in his chest unsettled him.

Isabelle uttered hardly a word as they climbed through the rolling greenery, past the ramshackle dairy farms and single-stoplight hamlets of southeastern Vermont. Her Automobile Association tour book, from which she'd quoted relentlessly the previous day, lay untouched atop the dashboard of the Oldsmobile. Lewinter reached for his wife's hand. She drew hers into her lap. Soon enough, he recognized, her seething would explode into outright fury.

"Hager's Corners," he ventured. "Isn't that where *Our Town* takes place?"

"That's *Grover's* Corners," said Isabelle, clipped and icy.

"I thought Martians landed in Grover's Corners. Didn't Orson

Welles get fired for reporting that Martians had landed in Grover's Corners, New Jersey?"

Isabelle's shoulders stiffened. "Grover's *Mill*. And Welles wasn't fired."

"Okay. Welles wasn't fired."

"And how could you be so irresponsible?" Isabelle demanded. "Didn't I tell you we should use a broker like everybody else? Why do you do everything ass-backwards?"

Lewinter kept his eyes focused on the vehicle ahead, a tandem trailer towing a powerboat, its wheels struggling with the high-grade turns. He said nothing. Once Isabelle generalized from a particular fault to "everything," his best defense was to hunker down and let her blows land where they might.

"Ass-goddamn-backwards," she repeated. "Uncle Harry was generous enough to leave us some of the most beautiful land on the planet, and all you have to do is go to a realtor and buy a house, and you can't even get that right."

Isabelle's logic, of course, was convoluted: a home purchased through a realtor would have come attached to its own property. Using her uncle's land required either relocating an existing house or erecting one from scratch. Lewinter chose not to mention these inconsistencies, nor did he point out that her "generous" uncle—a man whose psychiatric affliction, while never formally diagnosed, was instantly apparent to all who met him—had died intestate, leaving the property to them by default *after a tedious sojourn in probate court.* Instead, he heeded the GPS and eased onto a steep, shingly lane shadowed with conifers.

"And what about Frank?" she continued, her voice rising in volume and pitch. "How can you expect anything of him when you're too lazy to call a real-estate agent? Did it never once cross your mind that you have some iota of fatherly duty to set a good example?"

That was what was really eating at Isabelle, he knew. Their youngest had left college to spend a year on a desert retreat in Nevada, studying the art of traditional drum carving. The boy wasn't asking them for money, and on the telephone he sounded genuinely happy, if a bit clueless. But the uncertainty surrounding his future was killing his mother, minute by minute.

"I do the best I can," Lewinter said.

"The best you can? Is that all you have to say?"

Fortunately, according to the GPS, they'd reached their destination. To Lewinter's relief, the timberframe ranch house stood only twenty yards away, beckoning them across a lupine-tufted meadow. One solitary poplar towered adjacent to the dusty drive, its gnarled branches speckled with starlings. In the distance, the slate-blue peaks of the White Mountains melted into the horizon. Someone—maybe the manufacturer—had done the kindness of furnishing the post-and-beam porch with a rocking chair. Not even the airbrushed photos in the catalog had prepared Lewinter for the perfection of the structure.

"Here we are," he announced. "Home sweet home."

And he'd already eased the Oldsmobile into the drive when he caught sight of a clothesline connecting the poplar to the porch rail, and then a buxom, gray-haired woman hanging garments from a basket.

⌘

"I'LL TAKE CARE of this," Lewinter said. "I'm sure it's a misunderstanding."

"Or a crystal-meth den," Isabelle rejoined. "Or a brothel."

They'd parked halfway up the drive; their approach scattered the starlings. Outside, the air hung damp under the early morning sun. The gray-haired laundress stashed her basket on the porch and approached them. She wore a jonquil above her left ear and carried herself with an aura of proprietorship. She was clearly *living* in their house.

"Sorry to bother you," Lewinter said, "but I'm afraid there's been a mix-up."

Even as the words left his mouth, he was swept with the unsettling realization that he knew the soft-featured woman who stood arms akimbo between him and his dwelling.

"Allen Lewinter," she declared. "As I live and breathe."

"Kitty Canaday?"

That elicited a broad smile from the laundress. "I don't think anyone's called me Kitty in a couple of centuries," she said. "And I'm Catherine *Conrad* now."

"You're married?"

Lewinter heard the surprise in his own voice—although there was no earthly reason why Kitty Canaday, whom he hadn't laid eyes upon since college, shouldn't have married. How could he have expected otherwise? Yet somehow she'd remained frozen in his mind as the twenty-two-year-old coed who'd urged him to postpone medical school for the joys of communal living in the North Woods of Maine.

"Divorced," Kitty replied. "But I kept Phil's name so I could tell people I got something out of the relationship."

"Was it *that* bad?"

Kitty shrugged. "We had our ups and downs," she said. "Who doesn't? But in our case, we ended on a down note...."

Lewinter sensed his wife's eyes boring into the back of his skull. "This is my wife, Isabelle," he said rapidly. "Kitty and I were up at Cornell together."

"It's a pleasure to meet you," Kitty said.

Isabelle cleared her throat. "For the love of God, Allen. I didn't drive six hours for a college reunion." Her voice sizzled. "You work this out," she added, without even acknowledging Kitty. "I'm waiting in the car." Moments later, the door of the Oldsmobile shattered the alpine calm.

"I'm sorry," Lewinter said. "She's off her meds."

He regretted the words as soon as he said them. Why should his wife's mental health be any business of Kitty's? More unsettling was how easily he'd betrayed Isabelle, even in this minor way, to a woman

THE CURRENT OCCUPANT

he hadn't seen in forty-two years. *And* he'd been relieved to learn her marriage had failed. There was no denying it.

Schadenfreude, he assured himself. Nothing more.

"What I've actually come about is…."

Kitty waited patiently, her eyes poised on the verge of laughter, as though anticipating the punchline of a joke she'd already heard.

"Our house," Lewinter said. "This is our house."

And now Kitty—Catherine—did laugh. Her delight quivered over her breasts and hips like an earthquake cascading through cranberry sauce.

"I don't see what's so funny," snapped Lewinter, as he'd done countless times before, lounging on the Arts Quad at Cornell, as they'd argued over politics and war. Kitty might have been the only person on earth who'd ever found the Tet Offensive amusing. "Isabelle and I bought this house through a catalog and it seems to have been…misdelivered."

"That explains a lot," said Kitty. "I was wondering where it came from."

Lewinter resisted the urge to ask her how she'd ended up living in their house. Isabelle was right: This *wasn't* a college reunion. Why his ex-flame was squatting on his hard-earned timbers shouldn't be his concern. "So anyway," he said. "We'd like to have it back."

His request carried across the meadow. Behind him—he dared not turn—he felt the full bloom of Isabelle's rage. Overhead, a lone hawk glided on the currents.

Kitty shook her head. "You're out of luck."

"Excuse me?"

"I don't mean to cause you any trouble, Allen," Kitty said, "but I'm afraid it's my house now. You see, I've lived on this land for fifteen years—in a lovely old farmhouse dating from Ethan Allen's days—and then last month I went to visit my sister in Phoenix, and I came home to this…." She waved her fleshy arm, embracing the house in its arc. "My neighbor says your people tore through the old place with a wrecking ball and carried the debris away in dumpsters."

"You can't be serious? Why didn't anybody stop them?"

"Vermont folks mind their own business," Kitty said. "That's what I like about them. Usually." She retrieved her plastic basket from the porch. "I was upset at first. Especially about losing my stuff. But I'm adjusting. Telling myself to think of this as a long-overdue spring cleaning. You can laugh at me, if you like, but I believe in signs and omens. Deeply. If the universe wants me to live in a modern house, instead of a colonial one, who am I to question? And now that you're here, I'm *certain* there's meaning in all of this...."

"It is a strange coincidence," Lewinter conceded.

"I don't believe in coincidences. Things happen for reasons."

She rested the laundry basket on her hip, her face aglow. Was she flirting? And what did it matter if she were? "Again, I'm sorry for the inconvenience. If you have no place to go, you're welcome to stay. For as long as you need. Your wife, too...."

The situation left Lewinter flummoxed. "That's all right. We have to get back to New York...."

"We're both very lucky, you know," Kitty said.

"Lucky?"

"A lot of people would have sued you over what happened. *Most* people. Honestly, anybody else but me. So we should both consider it a blessing that the universe delivered your house to my doorstep, so to speak."

Before he'd had a chance to respond, or even reflect, an automobile horn bugled across the landscape like a battle cry. Kitty grinned. "So good to see you," she said, and returned to stringing clothes, leaving Lewinter to savor his good fortune.

❧

THE CURRENT OCCUPANT

ISABELLE FOUND NOTHING in the situation to feel grateful about. Once she'd learned how Kitty Canaday had come to occupy the dwelling, she gave Lewinter the silent treatment from the Massachusetts Turnpike to the Cross Bronx Expressway—three solid hours of frost. Several times, he attempted to distract her with remarks about the countryside, and the volume of city-bound traffic, and their daughter's upcoming baby shower, but she glowered at him and scowled. When they reached the Manhattan tolls, his wife slammed her tour book against the front of the glovebox.

"Aren't you going to say something?" she asked.

"What do you want me to say?" Lewinter, road-soaked and drowsy, fought back his own irritation. If Isabelle had found herself in Kitty's shoes, she'd have sued his pants off.

"You could begin by apologizing," Isabelle said.

He inched the Oldsmobile through the toll plaza. Dusk was descending. Once he'd garaged the car, it would be too late for a jog.

"Okay, I'm sorry. I didn't mean to upset you."

His wife hissed air between her clenched teeth. "Damn it, Allen. You don't even know what you're sorry for."

That was true. But nothing unusual.

"I'm sorry I bought a house from a catalog," he said. "It was lazy and shortsighted, and I wish I could take it back."

"You're *so* missing the point. How naive do you think I am? Do you really think this is about some lousy house in the country?"

"Isn't it?"

"This is about that—that *woman*," but the word could easily have been *whore* or *slut*. "Do you actually expect me to believe that if anybody else had commandeered our house, you'd have shrugged your shoulders and walked away?"

"Kitty didn't *commandeer* anything," Lewinter answered, maybe too quickly. "It was an honest mistake."

"Like hell it was," Isabelle cried. "Like Hiroshima was an honest mistake. Like Auschwitz was an honest-fucking-mistake."

Lewinter glanced at the nearest traffic, afraid his wife's voice might carry through the windows, wanting to assure passing motorists that Isabelle had grand-aunts, and a slew of cousins, who'd died in the camps. Nobody had heard her. The young couple in the next car appeared to be locked in a shouting match of their own.

"I can't believe you let her keep the house. *Our* house," Isabelle said.

"What did you want me to do? Haul it away on my shoulders? I'll phone the dealers in the morning and tell them what happened. I'm sure they'll want to avoid litigation; Kitty might not plan to sue, but they don't know that. If we're lucky, they'll refund our money and let her keep the house."

"What if they won't refund our money?"

"They will. Trust me, Isabelle. It's all going to work out," he promised, his own confidence increasing as he spoke. "And next time, I'll call a realtor."

❧

HE DUCKED OUT of the operating suite several times the following morning to phone the home manufacturer, as planned, but nobody at Modular Miracles answered. On his lunch break, he sent them an email that instantly bounced back: "Mailbox full."

"Why don't you try Brazil?" Isabelle jibed that evening. "Or Argentina? They're probably sitting on a tropical beach somewhere, courtesy of the Lewinter retirement fund, laughing their asses off at the guy who bought a mail-order house."

"I'll try again tomorrow. If that fails, I'll send them a certified letter."

"To where? Buenos Aires?"

Lewinter refused to let her gripes under his skin. All he wanted for his future—far more than a retirement home in New England—was a small measure of harmony. As the week progressed, and Isabelle's frustration mounted, he even contemplated phoning his wife's psychiatrist and pleading with the head-shrinker to intervene, although reedy, bespectacled Dr. Blauvelt, whom Lewinter ran into periodically at the hospital, seemed no match for the unmedicated avalanche that was his beloved. Instead, at Isabelle's insistence, he called the Better Business Bureau. His complaint, he discovered, was one among dozens. Modular Miracles had filed for liquidation in bankruptcy court and folded up shop.

I'll tell Isabelle next week, he promised himself. *After the baby shower.* Rachel's daughter would be their first grandchild, and he didn't want to ruin it. But duplicity, even on a small scale, defied Lewinter's nature. Climbing into bed beside his wife that night, the television tuned to a documentary about aerial warfare, he couldn't hold back.

"I have bad news," he confessed. "You were right, and I was wrong."

Isabelle muted the television. "Not the first time and not the last," she said. "So which was it? Brazil or Argentina?"

"They filed for bankruptcy," said Lewinter.

Now Isabelle's expression sharpened. "You're serious?"

"It's not as awful as it sounds. I spoke to a lawyer at the attorney general's office. We can add our names to the list of creditors. We'll get something back…."

"My ass, we'll get something back." Isabelle pounded a fist into his pillow. Her glasses, braced atop her head, had bunched her hair into stray loops, and her flared nostrils lent her a flavor of madness. "Fuck your list of creditors. It's *our* goddamn house and we paid for it and we're going to take it back—even if we have to throw that *woman* of yours out a window. Am I making myself clear?"

Lewinter suppressed the urge to say, *That woman's name is Kitty.* Which wasn't even true anymore. "We can't just *take* the house," he pleaded. "Be rational, Isabelle. Even if it was the right thing to do, nobody is going to move a house while someone's inside it."

"Then chase her out. Get a court order." Isabelle folded her arms across her chest. "I swear to God, Allen, it's either me or her. As far as I'm concerned, letting that woman live in my house is no different than cheating. It's like having an affair, but without sex." She switched off the bedside lamp and slid down under the covers. Lewinter wondered if she was aware how ridiculous she sounded—how *unmoored*. "I don't want to fight," she said, "I just want my house back."

Isabelle drew her sleep mask over her eyes. She'd left the muted television playing; the bombing of Cambodia flickered over them both. Even fighting gravity, his wife's face remained stunning. She'd started with more natural gifts than Kitty, appearance-wise, and nobody could argue that she hadn't aged gracefully. Not that he'd chosen between them. Not directly. Kitty and her fantasies of the Maine Woods had receded into distant memory, a youthful indulgence, before his medical-school roommate fixed him up with his own fiancée's cousin. *I'm lots of things*, Isabelle had warned on their second date, swizzling her cocktail with vigor. *But easy-going is not one of them. If you want easy-going and down-to-earth, buy yourself a basset hound.* Lewinter's retort had been: *At least, you're self-aware.* They'd both been dead right.

જ

LEWINTER DID NOT GET a court order the following morning. Instead, since it was a Friday, he presided over his weekly journal club for the ophthalmology residents, then headed across town to his Lexington Avenue office to see private patients. By the time he arrived, both of his daughters had already phoned multiple times. This was Isabelle's version of calling in the cavalry. Lauren proved easy enough to placate with vague promises, but Rachel—who shared her mother's temperament—demanded concrete action.

"Put yourself in Mom's shoes," she urged, more a command than

THE CURRENT OCCUPANT

a suggestion. "You run into some ex-girlfriend after God-knows-how-many years, and suddenly you want to give her a *house*. How is she supposed to feel?"

"I'm not *giving* her the house," Lewinter protested.

"Then what *are* you doing?"

A long silence followed. One of Lewinter's receptionists had left the door to the examination suite ajar; in the waiting area, two women debated whether "hysterical blindness" actually existed. Lewinter coiled the phone cord in his fingers. "I'm trying to do the right thing," he said. "I *have* put myself in your mother's shoes. But I've also tried to imagine what Kitty Canaday must be going through. Suppose you came home one day and everything you ever owned was gone…. If some grossly irresponsible developer had knocked down your eighteenth-century farmhouse and replaced it with a house off a truck."

Lewinter believed he sounded reasonable and compassionate. He also recognized that reason and compassion were no match for the women of his family.

"You're not married to Kit-Kat Canaday," Rachel replied.

The Romanian nurse practitioner poked her head into Lewinter's office; he shooed her away. "I don't need you reminding me who I'm married to," he said. "And I honestly don't understand what the urgency is. It's not like we were going to move into the place tomorrow. I've already added our claim to the list of creditors. What's the problem with letting the process work itself through?"

"My baby shower, for starters," his daughter said. "Mom promised me she'd help with the centerpieces—and now we have less than a week, and she's too stressed to get out of bed. It's bad enough that you're letting Frank waste his life away…"

"Your brother is a grown adult—"

Rachel cut him off again, but he was no longer listening. What was the point? His daughter hadn't gone skinny-dipping in Lake Cayuga with Kitty Canaday at daybreak on an August morning, nor had she wrapped an arm around the shaking Kitty at her grandmother's funeral, after a nine-hour, snow-blind overnight drive from Ithaca to Conway, New Hampshire. Nothing he said would convince the girl to let Kitty remain in the house. And the reality of the matter was that Rachel and Isabelle probably had it right: if he'd found anyone other than Kitty freeloading on his property, sob-story or not, he'd have fought them for the structure, pine-floorboard-by-goddamn-pine-floorboard. But you can never love another human being the way you love your college sweetheart at twenty-two—and not wanting to throw a former paramour onto the street, or out a window, did not constitute adultery. *It just didn't.*

His NP appeared at the office door again, pointing at her watch. Daciana knew that she'd end up paying for his time on the phone with her own precious minutes after five o'clock. No doubt the waiting room was already a zoo. He heard the two women who'd been debating hysterical blindness now squabbling over the meaning of the adage hanging above the water cooler: *In the land of the blind, the one-eyed man is king.* That seemed a fitting motto for life, Lewinter reflected. Not just for ophthalmology, but for all occasions.

"Frank doesn't even *play* the drums," Rachel said. "Mom's not overreacting. You're *under*reacting. Like you always do."

"I'll discuss this with your mother tonight." He hung up, denying his daughter an opportunity to object.

ᏋᎧ

ISABELLE DID MANAGE to order the centerpieces that afternoon. Lewinter hardly had time to change into his dungarees before she insisted on showing him photos on her laptop. What did he think of the European-themed flower displays: an Eiffel Tower sculpted from hydrangeas, a Parthenon replica in anemone and fleabane? Rachel's mother balanced the computer atop their bedspread and clicked through the various floral replicas. She seemed calmer, but a tinge disinhibited, a sure sign she'd doubled down on her Valium.

"Very imaginative," Lewinter said. "You've outdone yourself."

"She will be an international child, after all. Almost an EU citizen."

That *almost* was so quintessentially Isabelle—the same *almost* that had defined Frank's admission to Princeton and Lauren's qualification for Olympic swimming. In this case, Rachel's husband, a copyright attorney, had inherited his mother's Swiss citizenship.

"What are you thinking?" Isabelle asked. "You don't like them, do you?"

Lewinter chose not to point out that she'd purchased the centerpieces *over the Internet*. Was that really any different from buying a house? Well, maybe. But the dealer could still go belly-up and ruin Rachel's shower—so it wasn't *that* different. Personally, he didn't see the need for centerpieces at all. They were hosting a baby shower, not a state dinner. But marriage is about choosing battles, not winning them. "I *do* like them," he said. "Even more important, I'm sure your daughter is going to like them."

"Which is your favorite?" Isabelle pressed, elbows braced on the bedspread, stockings scissoring the air. She pointed at the laptop screen. "This one? Or this one? Or this one?" Her words lapped into one another, her vowels loose and liquid. Now he was certain that she'd downed a second Valium. "Come on, Allen. What's your favorite?"

"I think they're all brilliant."

"Liar," Isabelle retorted, but with a smile. "My favorite is the Colosseum. They've used azaleas for the arcades and forsythia for the pilasters."

To Lewinter, the floral cylinder on the screen looked like a Bundt cake. At the same time, he was thrilled—and relieved—to find Isabelle in good spirits. If kitsch landmarks distracted his wife from Kitty and the house, he wouldn't complain. And then—without warning—she asked, "Are you happy?"

That was the medication speaking, transforming Isabelle from mordant to maudlin. On two Percocets, she'd want to cuddle. On three, she'd weep for hours.

"Happy enough," he said. Which was true. Wasn't it? He had a secure marriage, three healthy children, a steady income. For the son of refugees who'd arrived from Antwerp with fifteen Belgian francs between them, this was nothing to sneeze at. He could easily have ended up like Isabelle's hard-drinking baby brother, unemployed and unemployable at fifty-seven, or like his own younger sister, divorced from the same sponger twice.

"Do you know what would make me happy?" Isabelle asked.

"I'm afraid to find out...."

She tugged his arm, pulling him down beside her on the bed. "Do you remember how we were sitting here last month, talking about the house, arguing about upholstery and color schemes? Do you remember how *good* everything was?" She nuzzled his shoulder. "I'm sorry we've been fighting. I want things to be good again."

"Me, too."

Isabelle locked her bony fingers around his large ones. "I wish I could explain why this house is so important to me. It just is. Even if I am being unreasonable, can you *please* get a court order and force your friend to move out? For me?"

Lewinter heard the desperation in his wife's voice, a far harder sentiment to resist than suspicion or rage. And he was struck by how old she looked: beautiful, unquestionably, but beautiful *for a woman of a certain age*—an age when healthy people keeled over without warning from all varieties of illness. He placed his free hand over hers.

"How about a compromise. Why don't I go talk to her?"

She eyed him warily. "To what end?"

"I honestly don't know. Maybe we can work something out. And if I can't convince her, I'll get a court order."

"Promise?"

Lewinter nodded decisively and stood up. "Promise. I'll leave first thing in the morning."

He reached for the phone to cancel his Saturday squash match. He felt himself running on autopilot. On impulse, he asked, "Do you want to come with me?"

Isabelle frowned. "Not a good idea. If I see that woman again, I'll end up in jail."

✑

THE OVERNIGHT DOORMAN was still on duty the next morning when Lewinter retrieved the Oldsmobile from the garage and retraced their route back to Hager's Corners. Isabelle remained asleep. He'd pecked her on the forehead, but she'd merely rolled over and clutched a pillow to her nightgown. On the Interstate, traffic remained sparse: drawbar trailers hauling swap bodies, eighteen-wheelers, a station wagon crowned with a pair of bicycles. When he crossed into Vermont and paused for a complimentary cup of coffee at the welcome center, it was hardly ten o'clock. The notion struck Lewinter that Kitty might be out for the morning, or even away for the entire weekend. His plan to negotiate a deal could prove a fool's errand. He wasn't even sure what he'd be negotiating. Maybe he just wanted to see her a second time. Remarkably, Isabelle hadn't expressed an iota of jealousy about the trip. She knew her husband too well: he was as incapable of sleeping with Kitty as he was capable of giving her his house.

Maybe it was Isabelle's absence, or his own anxiety, but the last leg of the journey took considerably longer than he'd recalled. The distance between towns—if you could even call them towns—seemed best measured in eons, not miles. A wall of Jersey barriers narrowed the highway to one shoulderless lane. Lewinter rolled down his window, soaking in the wood-smoked air of the countryside. On the radio, the Everly Brothers crooned "Bye, Bye Love." Soon came the signs for the turnoff, then the white clapboard church and Ye Olde Syrup Shoppe and the low-slung grammar school with the farmers market in its parking lot. Countless places where Kitty might squander a Saturday morning. *How absurd to think she'd be home*, Lewinter reflected. Even in college, Kitty had her calendar booked with small-scale adventures. He was already chastising himself for his poor foresight as he approached Kitty's address—and spotted his former girlfriend knee-deep in the verdant scruff on the opposite side of the lane. She sported a pith helmet; binoculars dangled around her neck. Lewinter parked at the head of the drive.

"I had a premonition you'd come back," she called.

Kitty shuffled toward him; perspiration matted her blouse to her chest. How natural—almost feral—she looked in her habitat. What a mystery, Lewinter thought, that he'd been able to love a woman like this and also Isabelle.

"Warblers are passing through this week," Kitty explained. "Some marsh birds, too. A friend spotted a pair of bitterns down at Bragdon Pond."

"I didn't know you were a birdwatcher."

Kitty's eyes gleamed. "I wasn't. A lot happens in forty years."

They stood face-to-face. Lewinter found himself at a loss, aware that Kitty must be assessing him, too, judging his soft belly and hirsute ears. "You had a premonition?"

Kitty met his question with a laugh. "Why don't I tell you about it over a cold drink? I have lemonade and beer. My neighbor also left me a pear strudel."

"Lemonade is fine."

He followed her into the house. *His* house, he reminded himself, although it didn't *feel* like his house. In fact, it didn't feel like anybody's house: except for a few cartons stacked in the foyer and a threadbare sofa beached in the living room, the place stood largely devoid of furniture and personal effects. No photographs, no knickknacks. In the kitchen,

THE CURRENT OCCUPANT

which did contain a refrigerator and a folding table, the curtain rods ran naked above bare windowpanes.

The kitchen contained only one chair.

"Sit down, please," Kitty instructed.

She retrieved a pitcher of lemonade from the refrigerator and poured him a glass.

"My neighbors have been extremely generous," she observed. "I was afraid I'd have to dip into my savings, but not a day goes by without someone dropping off a used appliance or a box of utensils. It's uncanny what Vermonters have collecting dust."

Lewinter surveyed the wallpaper, the countertops—pink granite, Isabelle's preference. How fresh and sterile everything seemed. An African violet on the windowsill offered the sole hint of a permanent human presence. He sipped his lemonade.

"I know what you're thinking," Kitty said. "Please don't feel that way. What's done is done. And it's quite liberating, really."

"You take life as it comes, don't you?"

"What else can I do? I try to look at the upside. No more dry rot. No more carpenter ants. I practically had a menagerie of ants and millipedes and beetles in that old place...."

Kitty leaned her rump against the counter, between empty sockets carved to house Lewinter's future oven and dishwasher. It was easy to picture her at home in her colonial farmhouse, stoking coals in winter, churning her own butter.

"How did you end up here?" Lewinter asked, because he enjoyed the mellow rhythms of her voice, but also to delay the start of their "negotiations" over the house.

That seemed to be the question she'd wanted. She launched into a narrative of her life—from her six months spent in the Maine wilderness, which proved far colder than any of her comrades had imagined, through her two decades with Phil Conrad, to her fifteen years in Hager's Corners, where she still worked part time in the county athenaeum. Along the way, she'd managed a food pantry in Portsmouth, New Hampshire, and a women's health clinic in Lowell, Massachusetts. Her ex-husband, who'd died shortly after their divorce, paid his bills installing septic tanks.

"But Phil was a potter," Kitty said. "You name your medium and he could spin you a flawless vessel. It was a remarkable gift. I wish I still had some photographs to show you...."

Kitty appeared as though she might laugh—or weep—he couldn't tell. "It sounds like you've led an exciting life," Lewinter said. It was something to say.

"I have, I suppose. And you?"

He'd known it was only a matter of time before she asked about him, before he had to shift their conversation toward less pleasant matters. "Exciting enough," he said. "What's that Chinese curse? May you live in interesting times."

Kitty retrieved his empty glass. "So they say. I believe the actual expression in Mandarin is: 'Better to live as a dog in an era of peace than a man in times of trouble.'"

He considered inquiring if she spoke Mandarin, whether this were another of the developments he'd missed over four decades. But he didn't. It was already three o'clock, and he could picture himself returning to Isabelle empty-handed. "I hate to change the subject," he said, "but we need to talk about the house. We have to figure something out."

Kitty nodded. "Is that why you've come back?"

"We're planning to retire here," he said. "To be blunt, Isabelle wants me to get a court order to put you on the street."

"And will you?"

Lewinter was amazed at how calm she remained in the face of his threat, as though they were discussing strangers. She washed his glass in the sink and set it on a dishrag to dry.

"What choice do I have?"

Kitty turned to face him again. "We all have choices."

"Such as…."

Her eyes locked on his—gentle, yet intense—the sort of expression one might wear when explaining death to a young child. He didn't dare look away.

"You could stay here," she said. "With me."

Her words settled over the room like a blanket.

"I told you I had a premonition," she said. "You came all this way for a reason. If all you wanted was to give me notice, you could have called. Or sent your lawyers…."

Kitty stepped toward him. "It's not the Maine Woods. But it's close. Just warmer." And she flashed him a smile.

Her visage was soft, welcoming. He realized that he was smiling, too.

"I should be going," he said. Lewinter stood up. "I'm sorry."

"Nothing to be sorry about," Kitty said. She was already Caroline Conrad once again—kindly, yet stoic. "I'll pack you some strudel for the road."

ৎৎ

LEWINTER RETURNED HOME after dark that evening. Again, too late for a jog. Isabelle was waiting for him in their bedroom, still wearing her bathrobe. Another of her military documentaries blazed fiercely on the television.

"Well?" she asked.

He stepped into the bathroom and splashed cold water on his face. His lower back ached from twelve hours behind the wheel.

"Well?"

He shook his head. "I'll call a lawyer tomorrow."

And he did.

He phoned the attorney who'd handled both of his sister's divorces, who in turn referred him to a family lawyer in Vermont, who ultimately recommended a property expert with offices in Manchester and Rutland. Everybody sympathized. They promised rapid action. It turned out the property expert had a longstanding relationship with a transport firm that could relocate the structure quickly for a modest fee.

"You're looking at a week, ten days, tops," the lawyer pledged. "Open and shut." Not once did Lewinter mention his prior connection with Kitty.

By the following Sunday, loading his Oldsmobile with floral landmarks for the baby shower, Lewinter had assurances that the matter would be settled that afternoon. In his mind, he pictured Kitty Canaday standing on her lawn, possibly holding a plastic basket containing her few remaining possessions, watching his outfit hook her new house to a rig. How disappointed Kitty looked—but how calm, how dignified. He watched helplessly as she shuffled into her van and set out to seek her fortunes on a neighbor's couch. In Lewinter's own vehicle, Isabelle shouted into her phone, shredding the caterer for his rampant incompetence.

"What the hell do I need with an ice cream cake?" his wife raged. "My daughter can't tolerate dairy. Am I making myself clear? Do you want her to have a miscarriage?"

Lewinter could easily envision Kitty laughing at Isabelle's frustration. He bit his own lip to stifle a guffaw.

"You'll be happy to know we got a court order," he informed Isabelle. "They'll have the house back in Hager's Notch by dinner."

"Is now really the time?" she demanded. "Jesus. What is wrong with you? You're about to have a granddaughter. Get your priorities straight."

Isabelle punched numbers into her phone again, while Lewinter imagined Kitty, unfazed, knocking on the neighboring farmhouse. He wanted to call after her. He experienced a yearning to tell her that he'd been wrong. *Both times*, he'd been wrong. But she'd retreated into her neighbor's dimly lit vestibule, and already his urge was lifting,

THE CURRENT OCCUPANT

evaporating in a sweat of snags and consequences. Once they reached the baby shower, Lewinter told himself, he'd have a vodka gimlet, or possibly two, and dance with each of his daughters, and soon this impulse, like so many others, would pass harmlessly into the night. •

The Topless Widow of Herkimer Street

QUINCY'S MOTHER HAD TAKEN his stepfather's death reasonably well, or so it seemed, so he was genuinely surprised when Lance Otten phoned in a huff. Otten was his mother's next-door neighbor, a retired accountant who once sued Quincy's dad over a basswood tree that had toppled across the property line. His call broke the calm of a sweltering Sunday afternoon in late June—less than twenty-four hours before oral arguments in Quincy's big copyright appeal—a day when Quincy needed a hassle from an overweight bean counter like he needed a turpentine enema. That's why he'd sent his wife and daughters to the waterpark in Richmond for the morning, planning to review his case briefs in their absence, but their trip had been cut short when his ten year old vomited atop the log flume. Now Gretchen was ensconced at the kitchen table, teaching the girls how to make shaved ice. "Your Ma's still out there," Otten complained. "And let me tell you, it's no pretty sight."

"I see," Quincy said. "I'll be over as soon as I can. Half an hour, at most."

"I'm doing you a favor, for old time's sake. I could have called the cops," added Otten. "My son and his fiancée are coming for supper. I can't have some batty old loon flashing her saggy tits in their faces."

"I *said* I'll take care of it," Quincy promised.

"You do that. Because if you don't, I'll have to."

Quincy hung up the receiver quickly, relieved to be off the line. His wife looked at him with her probing slate eyes, demanding to know the extent of the calamity.

"Mom is sunbathing topless on the patio," he said.

Gretchen shrugged. "It's not the end of the world." She had been raised in Amsterdam, the daughter of a career diplomat. She had a much higher threshold for shock than the family-oriented denizens of Herkimer Street in Laurendale, Virginia.

℘

THE HOUSE IN WHICH QUINCY had grown up, an ornate nineteenth-century Victorian with a wrap-around portico and a mansard roof, had initially stood upon several acres of open country near the outskirts of the city, but by the time Quincy's father had purchased the place— on the same GI Bill that put the elder Quincy T. Marder through law school—the land had been divided and subdivided repeatedly like the cells of a honeycomb. Low-slung, California-style bungalows now crowded the dwelling on three sides. All that remained of the property's former grandeur was its expansive front yard, fringed with forsythia blossoms and shaded by a luxuriant Dutch elm that had somehow escaped the blight. As a boy, Quincy had lost countless baseballs beneath the dense azalea hedge that encircled the porch; during high school, he'd pledged his love to half a dozen girls on the wrought-iron bench within the gazebo. In the wake of Otten's phone call, he charged up the flagstone path as though fleeing a bull, unlocked the front entrance with his own key, and crossed quickly through the foyer and dining room to the panoramic plate-glass doors that opened onto the wooden veranda. Sure enough, there was his mother, sunning herself on a chaise longue with a bottle of imported water in one hand and a romance novel braced against her knees. Ilene Marder-Marcus sported the same lime-green sun visor that she wore for golf, and a pair of perfectly tasteful beige slacks. From waist to throat, she was naked as a jaybird.

Quincy averted his gaze and knocked on the glass.

His mother looked up, startled. When she recognized Quincy, she bookmarked her novel and beckoned for him to join her on the deck.

"I didn't expect to see *you* today," she said breezily. "I thought you had a big case."

Quincy focused his eyes squarely on his mother's face, but he was unable to prevent her withered bronze body from encroaching upon the periphery of his gaze. In her nakedness, she revealed a complex and intimate history—not just flaccid breasts, but a faded Cesarean scar, the three bleached marks from her gallbladder surgery, angry vestiges of a childhood grease fire that had scalded her left shoulder.

"Can you please put something on?" Quincy asked.

"Good heavens, *you're* a prude these days," replied his mother. To Quincy's relief, she slid into a silk dressing gown with a Geisha print. "If you don't want to see a middle-aged woman *au naturel*, you shouldn't sneak up on her." She tightened the robe's belt, looping the ends into a bow. "How's Gretchen? How are the girls?"

"Gretchen and the girls are fine," said Quincy. "Look, Mom. We really need to talk."

"Okay. Talk."

Quincy drew a deep breath. Reasoning with his mother, he'd discovered soon after he learned to form his first sentences, was like straining the Sahara Desert through a sieve. "Lance Otten rang me up this afternoon," he said. "He's concerned that you're—well—he's upset about you sitting out here topless."

"*That's* what you're worked up about?" Ilene brushed away his complaint with the back of her hand. "You had me worried it was something serious."

"This *is* something serious. You're apparently quite visible from his downstairs windows. He's threatening to phone the police."

"So let him. Who's going to arrest a seventy-six-year-old widow for taking her blouse off in her own back yard?"

Ilene flashed him the same bemused, insouciant smile that had earned her a place on the cover of the May 1952 issue of *Harper's Bazaar*—the year before an ambitious and dashing young law student named Marder had carried her off to a backwater university town. On a woman in her seventies, this carefree look struck Quincy as disturbingly unhinged. Behind his mother, a pair of squirrels romped along the branches of a blooming crabapple.

"*Please,* Mom. Don't make a life-and-death issue of this," Quincy pleaded. "The neighbors have rights, too."

"*He's* the one making an issue out of this," Ilene shot back. "You don't hear me threatening to call in the National Guard when he mows *his* lawn with *his* shirt off."

"That's different." Quincy felt his frustration mounting. "You *know* that's different."

"How exactly is that different? Because some Puritan once decided that it's all right for Lance Otten to wander around town with his pot belly hanging out for all the world to admire? But if I want to enjoy the warmth of the sun on my skin for a few hours before I die, that's a hanging offense?" Ilene leaned forward, suddenly grim. "I didn't sunbathe out here when your stepfather was alive because he asked me not to. Wesley could be something of a prig, God bless his soul. You should've seen the look on his face that first time we visited the French Riviera. But I'm on my own now, Quincy Thomas Marder Junior, and I'm going to do as I wish on my own private property."

Quincy removed his glasses and rubbed the tension from the bridge of his nose. "Well, I tried my best to convince you."

"Yes, you did. Now, since you've driven all this way, would you like to stay for supper? My mahjongg set is coming over—we're ordering in

THE TOPLESS WIDOW OF HERKIMER STREET

sushi from that new Japanese restaurant on Patrick Henry Street—but you're welcome to join us."

Quincy shook his head. "I have an oral argument to prepare for." He crossed the deck and, already gripping the handle of the sliding door, attempted one last salvo. "How about if we build a fence? I'll pay for it."

"If Lance Otten wants a fence," she snapped, "let him build it on *his* property."

She folded her arms over her chest, making clear that she'd expressed her final words on the subject, and Quincy retreated across the dimly lit dining room and through the front door of the house. The lush aroma of peonies hung in the late afternoon air. A nuthatch pecked its way down the trunk of the elm. As Quincy was about to unlock his Cadillac, he heard a greeting from the adjoining lot. Mrs. Mahoney, who lived on the other side of Quincy's mother from Lance Otten, had taught him in the fourth grade.

"I knew I recognized you," she said. "How's your mother?"

"Fine. As indomitable as ever."

"That's good to hear," the retired teacher said. "How long has it been? Four months?"

"Nearly six," Quincy said.

His mother's second husband had died on Christmas morning. An aortic aneurysm.

"She's a trouper, your mother is," Mrs. Mahoney said. "Honestly, I was beginning to worry about her. Sometimes things have a way of unraveling when you're on your own. I suppose I shouldn't say this, but last weekend I had my niece and her sons over for a picnic, and your mother was sunning herself *topless*." The elderly woman dropped her voice to a whisper when she said the word *topless*, as though she were saying *cancer* or *divorced*. "I don't want to make a fuss, you understand, but boys that age are impressionable."

"Don't you worry," Quincy lied. "It's all under control."

NOTHING WAS EVEN REMOTELY under control, of course, where Ilene Marder-Marcus was concerned, and the following Saturday it was Sergeant Cross, of the Laurendale Police Department, who telephoned Quincy. The gravel-voiced cop had apparently been out to Herkimer Street that morning, but hadn't actually *seen* "the perpetrator" exposed—a requirement for a charge of misdemeanor indecency in Virginia. He hoped that a courtesy telephone call might forestall future episodes.

"We've received multiple complaints," he explained. "We'd prefer not to issue a summons, you understand, but this is a family-oriented community."

"I appreciate the heads-up," Quincy replied. "It won't happen again."

Gretchen entered the kitchen a moment later, carrying a laundry basket. A bottle of detergent crowned the soiled clothes heap like a figurine atop a wedding cake. She set the basket on the countertop and began transferring plates from the sink into the dishwasher.

"*What* won't happen again?" she inquired.

"I won't get a few minutes of peace, that's what." Quincy poured himself a glass of Chablis, even though it was only noon. "My mother is entertaining the neighbors again."

"She's just trying to reassert her identity," said Gretchen, who still worked part time as an adolescent psychologist. "That's only natural after a long marriage. I'll never understand why Americans are so uncomfortable with their own bodies."

Quincy wrapped his arms around his wife's waist and kissed her on the lips. "You make everything sound so simple."

"What's *not* simple?" asked Gretchen, glowing. "If you don't want to see something, you shouldn't look." She peeled Quincy's fingers from her hips, as though amused by the antics of a wayward child. "I'm not a lawyer, but it seems to me that the burden of resolving this ought to fall upon your mother's neighbors. *They're* the ones with the problem."

"That," he replied, "is *why* you're not a lawyer."

When considering the matter rationally, Quincy recognized that his mother had the better half of the argument. It *was* her property, after all. Moreover, while he was certainly no radical—his politics were more "don't rock the boat" than ACLU—he didn't exactly view a glimpse of exposed cleavage as a threat to public morality or the social order. But he also understood that cold logic wasn't the be-all and end-all in life. What he really couldn't comprehend was why everybody, on both sides, cared so much—his mother, Lance Otten, the Laurendale police. Didn't these people have larger fish to fry? For his own part, he had neither the time nor the energy to battle city hall. He'd caught a break when opposing counsel in his copyright case had requested a fifteen-day continuance, but he wasn't likely to have such luck again. If he had any chance of winning his appeal, this trouble with his mother required a permanent fix, not merely a patch to get them through another week. Quincy was reflecting on this predicament, nursing his wine and listening to the hum of the dishwasher, when his racing mind stumbled over the roots of a solution. The idea was daffy, yet brilliant. Five minutes later, he was on the telephone with Lance Otten, offering to *pay* the accountant to construct a fence.

"I don't know about this," said Otten. "I don't want to set any precedents. Once you lawyers gain a foothold, you'll make off with everything that's not nailed down."

Quincy resisted the urge to tell the accountant where to stick his precedents. "I'm trying to find some common ground here," he persisted. "Consider this a windfall. You name your price—anything reasonable—and we'll make it happen."

Lance Otten tossed out a number. It *wasn't* a reasonable number—Quincy could probably have raised a dome over his mother's house at that price—but as the managing partner at Randolph, Marder & Pastarnak, it was a figure that he could afford.

"You drive a hard bargain," Quincy said. "I'll write you a check and make the arrangements. Just please don't tell my mother who's footing the bill."

"Here's a deal for you," answered Otten. "I won't tell your Ma, if you don't tell my ball-and-chain how much you're shelling out. I love my wife as much as the next guy—don't get me wrong—but I love my solvency, too."

"Agreed," said Quincy.

His phone calls to Mrs. Mahoney, and the third neighbors, a Venezuelan starter couple named Arcaya, went far more smoothly. He could have gotten away with paying them far less than he'd paid the accountant, but that didn't sit right with him, and there was probably a special inferno in hell reserved for men who shortchanged their former elementary school teachers.

"I suppose good fences make good neighbors," Mrs. Mahoney had said—after repeatedly offering to let him erect the fence for free. "That seems like an awful lot of money, but if it's really the going rate, far be it for me to turn down an honest dollar." Unlike Lance Otten, Quincy had no choice but to reveal the true cost to his own wife.

"You only have one mother," said Gretchen. "I'll start making you bag lunches."

That was all the permission that Quincy required. When he arrived at the office on Monday morning, he personally phoned contractors out of the Yellow Pages until he found three willing to start work immediately. Each of the fences had to look different, after all, or his mother might suspect a conspiracy. He eventually settled upon a steel-palisade model for Otten's yard, a dry-stone hedge for Mrs. Mahoney's side, and a traditional red-brick wall to run along the rear border of the property. These barriers were to exceed seven feet in height, and with a few carefully placed merlons in the dry-stone, they would effectively block all of the sight-lines between the adjoining homes and Ilene's deck.

On Wednesday afternoon, Quincy did a quick drive-by. Already, the ridge of glistening palisades was visible from Herkimer Street. By the following Friday—the same morning he argued his appeal in the copyright dispute—two of the contractors had completed their labors, and the third had done everything except install a storm lamp requested by the Venezuelans. He was only a few hours away from visiting his mother, a duty he performed every other weekend, when the telephone disrupted his Saturday brunch. Since Gretchen had taken the girls to soccer practice—they were both part of the county summer league—and, as his wife had brought with her from Holland a European-inflected distrust of answering machines, the phone would continue to demand attention until either Quincy or the caller gave in. On the ninth ring, he stuffed the last of his bagel into his mouth and picked up the receiver.

"Quincy Marder?" asked the caller in an anxiety-flushed voice. "It's Gladys Mahoney. Your mother's neighbor."

"Is everything all right?" Quincy demanded, nearly choking. "Is Mom hurt?"

He had feared this call would come *someday*—but he'd always believed it was still years, and maybe even decades, away.

"Nothing like *that*, Quincy," Mrs. Mahoney said. "Nothing *medical*. But you really should come over here as soon as possible. *Immediately*, if you can."

"Why? What's going on?"

"It's hard to explain over the telephone," she replied. "I don't mean to sound mysterious, but I think it's best that you see this for yourself."

ℰℒ

QUINCY HAD WITNESSED many unlikely sights during his two decades as an intellectual-property attorney—including a pair of conjoined twins who'd sued each other over a family barbecue recipe—but nothing had prepared him for the scene he encountered on his mother's front lawn. At a distance, all that one could see was a handful of women seated inside the gazebo, their straw sunhats poking over the whitewashed parapet. But as Quincy hiked up the slight embankment that elevated his mother's yard above the street, he realized that three of these four elderly women, including his mother, were naked from the waist up. The fourth, a wizened creature with a frizz of over-hennaed hair, wore a turquoise bikini top that somehow rendered her flat chest even more indecent than the nudity of her peers. Exacerbating the absurdity of the tableau—transforming a moment of precociously senile rebellion into something fit for a Manet canvas—was the nonchalance with which the four women huddled around a folding table swathed with mahjongg tiles. Porcelain teacups rested on cork coasters. A crystal pitcher of lemonade sat at his mother's elbow. Quincy's arrival fell upon this lively affair like a wool blanket onto a blazing fire. One of the topless women reached for her blouse, but Quincy's mother shot her a fierce glare, and she drew back her hand.

"I figured you'd stop by, sooner or later," Ilene said.

She introduced her brood of hens to him. "Quincy, this is Estelle…and Dora…and Rosalyn. You might have known Rosalyn's son, Zachary—Zachary Steinhoff—he was in your class at Yale."

"Yale is a large school," retorted Quincy, aware of the pique in his voice. He didn't wish to be rude to these women, but he no longer possessed the forbearance for pleasantries, so he decided that the best course of action was to ignore his mother's friends entirely. "You've really crossed the line this time, Mom. Have you gone mad?"

Ilene rolled her eyes. "Did that Otten nitwit call you again in one of his states?"

"Deirdre Mahoney called me. Needless to say, she was concerned." He rested his gaze upon the mahjongg tiles, concentrating on their inscrutable code of circles and Chinese characters. It struck him suddenly that his own mother was a lot like a mahjongg square. "This is not normal behavior and you know it, Mom. Now would you please ask your friends to cover themselves up? At least while I'm here?"

Ilene's companions looked toward her for guidance, leaving no doubt that they were wholly under her thrall. She flashed a commanding grin.

"You sound like the Hays Code, Quincy. Quite frankly, there was a time not so long ago when an army couldn't have dragged your tiny mouth from my sore nipples." Ilene paused for her friends to appreciate her breastfeeding quip, obviously prepared in advance. Quincy felt his chest pounding. "Go ahead and blush," she continued. "But if you're uncomfortable, you have only yourself to blame."

"What's that supposed to mean?"

"It means," replied Ilene, each word animated with displeasure, "that your mother didn't fall off the hay wagon yesterday. I know who's paying for those ridiculous walls, and you had no business going behind my back like that."

"I was trying to be helpful."

"Well, you weren't. It's like a medieval ghetto back there now—not an ounce of sunlight gets in after two o'clock."

Quincy glanced nervously up Herkimer Street: a Dominion Resources utility truck stood vacant opposite the Carlyles' driveway; mourning doves perched atop the power lines. It was only a matter of time, Quincy realized, before toddlers on tricycles, or a busload of Cub Scouts, meandered onto the block. "Can we please talk this over inside?" he begged.

The faux redhead in the bikini top cleared her throat, looking anxiously from her companions to Quincy. "Maybe we should be going," she offered.

"Nonsense, Dora," Ilene declared. "Estelle, it's your turn to draw."

"Your old mother's got a bit of Cole Porter in her," the woman named Rosalyn explained, as though offering an apology. "She doesn't like to be fenced in."

Quincy's first instinct was to demand the phone number of Mrs. Steinhoff's own adult son—as though she were a misbehaved teenager to be reported. But these women were grownups, capable of making their own decisions, and he had no more power over his mother than he had over the Queen of England. The truth of the matter was that he'd always been his father's son: steady and dependable. He'd fallen for Gretchen because, beyond her Scandinavian beauty, she was the sort of rational, even-keeled mate who made the struggle of daily living easier. What compelled other men—his father included—to chase after tempestuous women had always puzzled Quincy, and even in his childhood, his mother's volatility had frightened him. And now it seemed as though the full force of her youthful caprice, suppressed during twelve years of an autumn marriage to Wesley Marcus, DVM, was roaring forth from behind a makeshift dam. These weren't matters that Quincy could discuss in front of three perfect strangers, obviously. As he yearned desperately for a way to break through to his mother, panic rising in his throat, a Laurendale squad car coasted to the curbside.

Sergeant Cross shuffled up the flagstone path. The cop was a pudgy, red-faced old-timer whose professional accoutrements—a belt laced with handcuffs, flashlight, and billy club—made him look like a grandfather decked out for a Boy Scouts reunion. He shook Quincy's hand vigorously, as though they'd been school chums.

"Ladies, ladies," the sergeant said. "You're binding my hands here. Like I told you last week, Mrs. M., you keep this up and you're going to face charges."

Quincy was amazed at the officer's casual bearing, so different from the hard-nosed sticklers who'd patrolled the town in his youth. "You'll have to forgive my mother, officer," he implored. "She lost her husband recently and—"

"Six months ago," Ilene interjected. "Don't make excuses."

"She's having a hard time of it," Quincy continued. "I'm sure that when she realizes that she could go to jail, she'll reconsider her antics. Won't you, Mom?"

An uneasy silence swept over the yard, punctuated only by the drone of distant traffic from the Interstate. The woman who had previously reached for her blouse, Estelle, held her plump arms in front of her cleavage. Ilene drummed her fingers on the card table.

"I'll tell you what I'm going to do," the sergeant said. "I'm going to take a cruise around the block. A long, slow cruise. I'm optimistic that when I pass by here again, I won't have any reason to get out of my vehicle."

"Thank you," Quincy said. "We really do appreciate it."

Cross shook Quincy's hand a second time and departed down the path. Quincy watched the cop's progress as though tracing the course of a retreating army. Within seconds of his squad car rounding the bend and disappearing behind the Carlyles' unkempt privet, an orange box-truck rolled down Herkimer Street from the opposite direction. Emblazoned along the side of the truck was what amounted to Quincy's own epitaph: WRIC-TV RICHMOND NEWS.

℘

MEMBERS OF THE "GRAY SOLIDARITY BRIGADE" began arriving in the early afternoon, mostly well-preserved matrons in their seventies and eighties. Some came alone, peering over the steering wheels of boat-like Cadillacs and Oldsmobiles more suited for raised blocks in a museum. Others appeared in pairs and trios, united for moral support. One lady brought along her husband—a blind psychiatrist with pendulous jowls and an English moustache, who quipped to the reporters, "Lucy said I could come with her if I promised not to look." By the time Sergeant Cross finally did return—his uniform shirt stained with tomato sauce— more than twenty-five elderly women had joined Quincy's mother on her front lawn. The newcomers displayed various degrees of undress, many preferring to keep on their brassieres, but at least ten of the protesters were fully topless, including a ninety-one-year-old retired librarian from Petersburg who claimed to be a grand-niece of suffragette

Emmeline Pankhurst. Quincy watched from the porch swing, powerless to intervene.

About an hour later, the first of the distraught children appeared. These were middle-aged men and women, much like Quincy, who had seen their mothers on the afternoon news or received calls from alarmed relatives, and had sped through every stop sign and traffic light between their own homes and Herkimer Street. Each re-enacted the same battle that Quincy had fought earlier, pleading and threatening in his or her own distinct way. A few managed to cajole their loved ones into departing, but the vast majority milled about the yard helplessly, attempting to keep their eyes above the sea of bare, spent flesh. Lance Otten emerged from his bungalow around two o'clock—sporting his trademark navy-blue leisure suit and Panama hat—and, ignoring Quincy entirely, spoke for a moment with several of the dozen officers who had joined Sergeant Cross at a temporary command center under the Dutch elm. This conversation soon acquired a heated tone— Quincy could not hear the words, but saw the anger suffuse across the accountant's blotchy cheeks—and ended with Otten throwing his hat on the grass in frustration. Meanwhile, Quincy's mother remained topless, chatting with local reporters and leading her motley band of followers in a raucous chorus of Marlo Thomas's "Parents are People." If Quincy had been watching these events unfold on the television screen, and if Ilene had been some other unfortunate sop's mother, he probably would have found the spectacle highly entertaining. But—to quote the expression that his elder daughter had picked up at summer camp—if grandmother had testicles, she'd be grandfather.

Quincy didn't dare approach the police, afraid this might spur them into action. Yet shortly after Otten departed, Sergeant Cross sat down beside Quincy on the porch.

"How you doing?" the cop asked.

"I could be better."

"Couldn't we all." Cross wiped his brow with his sleeve. "We're going to wait them out. They'll get tired. They'll go home. Better than dealing with the logistics of arresting them all. But I'm afraid I'm going to have to issue your mother a summons."

At least there'd be no SWAT team. No paddy wagon.

"What she really needs," Quincy said, "is a straitjacket."

"Hang in there." Cross patted Quincy on the shoulder and trundled off.

The rain rolled in a few minutes later, an afternoon lightning squall that started with large, sparse drops that oozed from the sky. One by one, Ilene's compatriots retreated to their Oldsmobiles and Cadillacs. Rosalyn Steinhoff's son hustled off his mother and the woman named Dora under a colossal black umbrella. The Laurendale police offered free rides home to willing protesters who lacked transportation. Eventually, only Quincy's mother remained, arms akimbo in the shelter of the gazebo. She stood stomach in, chest out, like a military recruit, while the surrounding storm lashed her bare back and cleavage with spray. Quincy sat on the bench beside her, watching the rain soak the mahjongg board. During a lull in the downpour, Sergeant Cross and another officer, a young man named Morton with a nickel-sized mole on his cheek, dashed from their patrol cars to the gazebo.

"Okay, Mrs. M.," Cross said. "We've all had our excitement for the day. Now why don't you go inside with your son, and once you've had a chance to put on some dry clothing, Officer Morton here will come back and write you a summons."

"I'm not going anywhere," Ilene answered. "It's a rainstorm, not the apocalypse. Do you expect me to melt?"

"Then I'm afraid I have to place you under arrest," Cross said. While Quincy looked on dumbfounded, the officer grasped his mother gently but firmly by the elbow and handcuffed her wrists. "You have the right to remain silent. We have no way of giving you a lawyer, but one will be appointed for you, if you wish, when you go to court…."

Ilene appeared unfazed. She followed Morton toward the squad car.

"You don't have to keep your eyes down like that, young man," she said to the junior policeman. "My bosom won't turn you to stone."

The sky responded with a resounding clap of thunder, a celestial sky-quake, as though the heavens themselves were affronted by Ilene's nudity.

ↂ

QUINCY TRAILED THE CONVOY of patrol cars to the Laurendale police headquarters, a sprawling and unsightly structure squeezed between Governor Harry F. Byrd Memorial High School and the stately, Federal-style county courthouse. He waited in the lobby while his mother went through booking and fingerprinting, then followed Officer Morton past a series of cubicles into a musty storeroom. Rows of modular shelves contained office supplies of disparate vintages, including stack upon stack of unopened carbon paper. Plastic bins held an armada of orange roadwork cones. Ilene sat on a folding chair beneath a small yet unbarred window, still bare-chested, her hands clasped neatly in her lap. On the opposite wall hung a katana saber, identified as a gift from the police prefect of Laurendale's "sister city" in Japan. Not an ideal heirloom, Quincy reflected, to leave within reach of a prisoner. Nearby, a female cop who appeared even younger than Officer Morton—Patrolwoman Barrett—scanned a glossy bridal magazine.

"Under the circumstances, Sergeant Cross didn't think that the holding pen was a workable option," Morton explained. "But if you could convince your mother to clothe herself, we would be mighty appreciative."

If grandmother had testicles, Quincy thought. He stood in the dim light, waiting for his mother to speak. She didn't.

"Well, Mom. Are you satisfied?" he demanded.

"Actually, I *am* satisfied. Now the courts can settle this business once and for all."

"There's nothing to settle. You broke the law." Quincy circled behind his mother's chair, so he wouldn't have to worry about viewing her breasts. "I have no idea what the penalty for misdemeanor indecency is in Virginia, but maybe if you apologize to the judge—*and you mean it*—you'll get off with a suspended sentence."

"I'm not apologizing for anything," Ilene snapped. "The law is unconstitutional."

"For God's sake, Mom. Enough already!"

"The law applies differently to women than it does to men," Ilene persisted. "You don't need any Ivy League law degree to realize that's fishy."

Quincy had no opportunity to present a rebuttal—to explain that gender discrimination was, in fact, sometimes both constitutional *and* legal. He'd hardly formulated his thoughts when Office Morton reappeared in the doorway.

"Your bail hearing is coming up shortly, ma'am. Would you like a few moments to speak with the public defender?"

"That won't be necessary," Ilene said. "I already have my own lawyer."

"And who is that?" Quincy asked.

"*You're* my lawyer," replied his mother, poking him in the sternum. "You created this mess, Quincy Thomas, and now you're going to clean it up."

Quincy felt self-conscious about bickering in front of the cops. Officer Barrett flipped through her magazine pages indifferently.

"This is ridiculous, Mom. I'm not even wearing a jacket."

"Borrow one. You're resourceful."

"But I'm not a criminal-defense lawyer. I'm not even *remotely* qualified to handle a misdemeanor charge."

"A lawyer is a lawyer is a lawyer. Your father would never have paid for you to go to Yale Law School if he'd known you would end up unqualified."

QUINCY CALLED GRETCHEN on his cell phone and implored her to bring his blue suit to the police station as quickly as possible. "Everything is fine, really," he promised. "Just my mother being my mother. Don't turn on the evening news, okay, and I'll fill you in over dinner." Twenty minutes later, still looping his tie while he walked, he crossed the varsity baseball field and entered the old wing of the public high school. This was where municipal trials were being held while the county renovated the courthouse. Judge Landau presided over misdemeanor cases in the same gym where Quincy had once played JV basketball. A curtain had been drawn around the court, covering the padded mats, and the backboards had been raised into the rafters, but the three-point line was still visible beneath the attorneys' benches. What a contrast to federal court in Richmond, where Quincy argued trademark law.

Judge Landau wore a tweed jacket and a bowtie, rather than a robe. He was an egg-bald, bespectacled man in his seventies, who looked as though he'd been roused from a nap. The public prosecutor—a woman half Quincy's age—asked that bail be set at $500.

"All in due course," Landau said. "Where is the defendant?"

"She waives her right to be present," Quincy explained.

"Let the record show that the defendant has waived her right to be present and enter a plea of not guilty," the judge instructed. "And what say you to $500 cash bail, counselor?"

Five hundred dollars seemed perfectly reasonable to Quincy, far less than he'd squandered walling in his mother's yard. But he was an attorney, acting on behalf of a client, so his own judgment was of secondary importance.

"With all due respect, Your Honor," Quincy said. "We'd like to have these charges dismissed at the outset. You see, it's my mother's contention that the statute under which she is being charged is unconstitutional and—"

"Hold on a moment, counselor," the judge interjected. He removed his glasses and wiped them with his handkerchief. "Am I to understand that your client is your mother?"

"Yes, that is correct, Your Honor."

"Very well. Proceed."

"It is my *client's* contention, Your Honor, that a statute which criminalizes nudity above the waist for women, but not for men, violates the due process clause of the Fourteenth Amendment." That sounded plausible, he assured himself. When neither the judge nor the prosecutor objected, he elaborated his claim—drawing upon the vestiges of his law school education, citing cases that hadn't crossed his lips in two decades. He invoked Thurgood Marshall, John Marshall, Blackstone's *Commentaries*. He wasn't one hundred percent certain that he had any idea what he was talking about—but the words rolled off his tongue, point by point, until he'd nearly convinced himself that his poor elderly mother was being done a grave injustice by a retrograde penal code. "So you have no choice, Your Honor," he concluded, nearly out of breath, "but to uphold the principle of gender equality enshrined in both the state and national constitutions, and to declare the statute in question null and void."

Quincy stopped speaking and looked around. The prosecuting attorney, who he now realized was a law student working under supervision, looked as though she'd been flattened by a fast-moving freight train. One of the bailiffs, a lantern-jawed man with a kente cloth draped over his uniform, gave Quincy a discreet thumbs-up. Judge Landau stared at Quincy, as though he might electrocute him with his gaze.

"That was quite interesting, counselor," the judge said suddenly. "Unfortunately, this is not a trial, but merely a bail hearing." He examined the contents of a manila folder, then reached for his gavel. "The defendant is released on her own recognizance, pending trial."

"Thank you, Your Honor," Quincy said.

"And one more thing, counselor," the judge said. "As a man who has a lovely wife who likes to sunbathe topless in her own backyard, I do wish you all the best of luck."

cɔ

QUINCY'S MOTHER WAS WAITING exactly as he had left her. Still topless. Still seated erect as a plywood board—a tribute to her modeling-school training. She was engaged in a lively chat with a new female guard, a middle-aged officer distinguished by her highly deficient chin. Quincy handed this officer the magistrate's order. The cop looked it over carefully, then instructed him to wait with his mother while she completed some essential paperwork.

Quincy slumped on the cop's stool, depleted. Only a pale film of twilight now filtered through the small unbarred window, and a gray dusk had settled over the storeroom.

"Well? Did we win?" Ilene demanded.

"You made bail, if that's what you're asking."

"But the law? Did they declare it unconstitutional?"

"It was only a bail hearing. Not a trial."

A furrow of disappointment deepened on Ilene's forehead. "Very well," she declared. "But don't you think for a second that I'm giving up."

She turned her chair to face his, challenging him to cross her.

"I'm sure you're not giving up," Quincy answered. "You'll probably fight your case all the way to the United States Supreme Court. But do you know what, Mom? I don't care."

"Don't mock me, Quincy. It's unbecoming."

"No. I mean it." He stood up, paced across the alcove. "You're a grown adult. If you want to go topless, that's your business. If you want to go around town bottomless, that's your business, too. Stage a burlesque show on the steps of the Methodist Church, if that's what inspires you, but I'm bone tired, and I haven't seen my daughters all weekend, and I really don't have it in me to worry about your stunts anymore."

Quincy met his mother's harsh gaze. A deadly hush fell between them. After one of the longest, most uncomfortable minutes of Quincy's life, Ilene looked away.

"Your grandmother, your dad's mother, she used to call them nice *eyes*," said Ilene, seemingly apropos of nothing. "If she wanted to say that a girl was well-endowed in the chest department, she'd say that the young woman had 'a delightful pair of eyes.' Alternatively, she might say a girl was 'not much to look at in the eye department.' I'd nearly forgotten…."

"Why are you telling me this?"

"So *somebody* will remember. After I'm gone," said Ilene, her voice now more wistful than defiant. "Do you know what I was thinking before, while you were in court? I was thinking that, soon enough, there won't be anybody around who has any memory of what my breasts even looked like." Quincy's mother smiled as though this notion amused her. "My breasts will be lost to history—like Joan of Arc's or Helen of Troy's."

Something in his mother's tone, something sad and distant, made Quincy uneasy.

"Would you mind if I borrowed your jacket?" Ilene asked. "I don't owe it to anybody to catch my death, now do I?"

Quincy passed her his jacket. The large coat enveloped her diminutive frame. As he watched her fastening the buttons over her pale skin, the realization entered his consciousness that the next time he saw her naked flesh, she might be lost to him forever. Already a tiny woman wrapped in a giant cloak, she looked decades older, sexless, nearly lifeless—her body the sort of breathing shell that you might pass on a public street without even taking notice. •

Lessons in Platygaeanism

O N OUR FIRST DAY at his cabin, when I was nearly eight and Oren had just turned ten, Uncle Rex sat us down for a man-to-man talk. This was Bear Claw, Alaska, in the summer of 1972—not the "postcard" Alaska of glacier-capped peaks and coniferous woodlands, but a rough-and-tumble fishing hub straddling the tundra. The cabin itself stood well upriver from the town. For many years, the structure had been nothing more than a wooden cube balanced atop a ring of cinderblocks. But that spring Uncle Rex had tacked on a makeshift deck (a spruce ledge, really, without a railing). Earlier in the morning, my mother had steered us across the mudfield that was her brother's front yard, hopping between mossy fence rails and warped spruce planks, warning us to mind our trouser cuffs. But as soon as Uncle Rex had us alone, he got down to business. "Listen up," he said, scratching his auburn beard. "I'm gonna tell you boys some sanity."

Uncle Rex paced with his back to the river. His broad shoulders held his meager flesh like a coat hanger, and despite his Coast Guard service, his bearing looked more scarecrow than military. Behind him, several bends up the Kuskokwim, the angular roof of the district jail poked over the aspen thicket like the dome of a giant pup tent.

"You ready for some sanity, boys?"

I looked at Oren. My new stepbrother sat perched on the rump of an overturned wheelbarrow, his expression curious and benign. At his feet lay a carpenter's level, a rubber mallet, and an assortment of drill bits.

"Afraid to talk, boys? Is that what my sister's done to you?" Uncle Rex lifted his canvas yachtsman's cap. He mopped his brow with the back of his sleeve. "I asked you boys if you're ready for some sanity."

Oren said nothing. The dogs—a pair of Samoyed mutts—yapped in their pen. "I guess so," I said.

"I guess I'll tell you, then," said Uncle Rex, grinning. He stepped toward us and lowered his heavy voice: "The earth," he said. "It's as flat as a plywood board."

The pronouncement didn't shock me. Maybe it was the even tone to Uncle Rex's words, but as likely it was the credulity of a boy who, as recently as New Year's, had been living alone with his mother in a ranch house outside of Anchorage. If my surroundings could flatten out suddenly, why not the planet?

"Okay," I said.

"Flat as a plywood board," he repeated. "That means you have to be careful."

"Careful," I agreed.

"Do you know *why* you have to be careful?"

I didn't. I shook my head.

Uncle Rex turned to Oren. "Do *you* know why you have to be careful?"

Oren kicked a stone across the deck. "Not to fall off the edge," he said.

"Not to trust received wisdom," Uncle Rex said. "Not to believe what they tell you about moon landings and Mariner probes, about Christopher Columbus. Damn that. Demand empirical evidence. Think for yourselves." He rested one foot atop the electric smoker and braced his forearm on his knee. "When your Aunt Caroline got sick, I was too much the fool to ask questions. Or at least the right questions. I swallowed all their rot about high-grade astrocytomas and bone metastases, those bigwig neurologists with their silver tie-clips. Do you know what I'm saying, boys?"

"Yes, sir," I lied. All I knew about Aunt Caroline was that she'd died long before I was born, and that she'd been a native Yup'ik, and that I wasn't to mention her to Uncle Rex.

"I hope you do, for your sakes." Uncle Rex fished his pipe from the pocket of his parka. He turned his back to the wind and held a match to the bowl—treating us to sweet, leathery gusts of tobacco. "Otherwise, you'll get your brain ladled out in scoops while they plumb for a tumor that's not there." He turned sharply and glared at Oren. "It was a vitamin deficiency, that's all. B-12 on account of her going vegetarian. A couple of chicken sandwiches, and all that numbness would have gone away."

Oren raised his eyebrows slightly, his hands folded in his lap. I still remember the detachment in his features, his rigid pose, all of him so hard and pale, like an alabaster caryatid. It's the same look he displays today, on television, defending his baboon experiments—but at seven years old it exacted my respect.

"After that, I got to asking other questions," said Uncle Rex, a tremor in his voice. "I read the Platygaenists—Anaximander and Cyril of Jerusalem and Dr. Rowbotham. The bottom line is that all this business about digging to China is a load of claptrap. Am I making myself understood?"

Oren kicked another pebble over the side of the deck. It landed in the water with a plunk. "Can we go there?" he asked.

Uncle Rex stiffened. "Where?"

"The edge."

A cloud of smoke rose from Uncle Rex's pipe. His face fogged over momentarily—the expression that later, after a series of minor strokes, would become his permanent mask.

"Can you take us to the edge of the earth?" Oren asked again.

"It's far away."

"How far?"

Uncle Rex frowned. "Very far, boy." For a moment he looked off toward the horizon—the broad, flat river and the scrub of willow and aspen beyond. Then he turned toward me and asked, "Are you ready to catch yourself some dinner?"

"Okay," I said.

I'd never been out on the river before—the Kuskokwim had only broken up a month earlier—but I followed Uncle Rex dutifully down the iron stairs to the boat launch. The Boniface's Revenge lay low in the water. It was a fifteen-foot aluminum johnboat with an Elgin outboard motor. Eventually, I would inherit this heirloom, and in high school it ferried me and any number of hapless girlfriends out to the secluded shallows of Dead Russian Cove. (Relating St. Boniface's condemnation of the Heresy of Vergilius—the assertion of the rotundity of the earth— became a standard of my teenage foreplay.) That morning, though, I drew my life jacket tight before stepping onto the sloshing frame. From the back of the boat, I could see Oren, in profile, still balanced atop the overturned wheelbarrow.

"You coming, boy?" shouted Uncle Rex.

He winked at me and revved the engine.

"In a minute," Oren answered. "I'm thinking."

☙

MY NEW STEPFATHER didn't take well to Uncle Rex's revelation. Mr. Cruikshank—whom I was supposed to call Papa, but never could—was a compact, muscular man with a sharp jaw, deep-set black eyes, and a shock of prematurely gray hair. On the Kenai Peninsula he'd been, at various times, a fire lookout, wildlife guide, fifth-grade teacher, alcohol inspector, and mate on the Seward-Cordova ferry, but in Bear Claw he earned a living fixing things. Boilers. Septic tanks. Prop-plane engines. Once, he even came to repair a leak in the roof of Miss Langley's classroom, and he'd removed the popcorn ceiling square by square, practically over our heads, while we constructed dioramas of the North Slope. Yet what I remember most of Artie Cruikshank was his smell—a blend of rust, wet dog, and turpentine. That, and his habit of eating apple slices off a paring knife. There may have been a glut of bachelors in Alaska during those first decades of statehood—what should have been a buyer's market for an attractive widow like my mother—but the wisdom went that while the odds were good, the goods were odd. By these standards, Oren's father, while in his own way obsessively fastidious, stood well within two standard deviations of the mean. He owned his own house. He didn't drink. In the Kuskokwim Delta, Cruikshank was a catch. I doubt this mattered to my mother, though. She already had a house, insurance money. Nor—although this may be a son's wishful thinking—do I think she remarried for love. What she'd needed, after my father's accident, was another body to look after. Someone whose errands to run on Sunday afternoons.

My mother had given up a lot to return to Bear Claw. In Anchorage, she'd been assigned to the Native Health Service Hospital—more or less a 9-to-5 gig. Out in the Delta, she was one of two optometrists for the entire district: Six thousand Yup'ik spread over three dozen villages. Bear Claw itself wasn't exactly a metropolis—that was before they built the regional medical center—but at least it had a supermarket, a movie theater, a café. The Yup'ik in the villages lived at subsistence levels. At best, one might expect a small general store; usually, only a modern clapboard post office surrounded by corrugated tin huts. Two weeks out of five, my mother puddle-jumped through communities like Upper Kalskag and Nightmute and Scammon Bay, adjusting prescriptions and diagnosing cataracts. During her three "off weeks"—at the local clinic— she lived with us in the one-story cylindrical house that the previous owner had purchased from a Montgomery Ward catalog. That's how, on summer days when school was out and Oren's father was off fixing things, we first found ourselves relegated to the supervision of my mother's older brother.

It was Oren who divulged Uncle Rex's unorthodox views. Not me. Three days later, after two more mornings of fishing and philosophy, my stepbrother broached the matter before supper, while my mother was filleting salmon and his father was standing on a step-stool, tinkering with the ceiling fan. "Uncle Rex says the earth is flat."

My mother smiled. "He's a character, isn't he?"

"Miss Langley told us that *nobody* believes the earth is flat anymore."

"Almost nobody, Oren," my mother said.

"Well, how do we know he's wrong?" Oren pressed.

Mr. Cruikshank descended a rung on the step-stool. In one fist, he gripped a hammer. He used the other hand to remove several nails from between his lips. "What's this about?" he asked.

"Uncle Rex taught us the platygaenists' theory of the earth."

A scar of dirty sweat cut across Mr. Cruikshank's brow. "Speak English."

"Platygaenism," Oren said. "The belief that the earth is flat."

Mr. Cruikshank wiped his face with his bare palm. "Kevin's uncle isn't right in the head. Don't believe anything the old coot says."

"So Miss Langley's correct?"

Mr. Cruikshank appeared suddenly disconcerted, slack-jawed. He stepped entirely off the ladder. "What's that?"

"I asked if Miss Langley was correct about Columbus?"

"Jesus. Of course she's correct."

"Can you prove it's round?" Oren persisted.

My stepbrother wasn't trying to be difficult, I now understand. The truth was that he worshipped his father—that he bragged constantly about the man's past accomplishments as a fire scout. I imagine Oren genuinely expected to be presented with conclusive evidence. Instead, his father scowled. Mr. Cruikshank now held the hammer in both hands,

LESSONS IN PLATYGAEANISM

and for a moment, it appeared he might break the handle over his knee. "I don't have to prove it," he said irritably. "It's already been proved."

My stepfather unhitched his work belt. It dropped to the carpet with a thud. After that, a tense silence descended upon the room, intensified by the pale gray light of evening. I watched Oren carefully, trying to size him up. He'd folded his slight arms over his striped shirt. His face was honed, but inscrutable.

Mr. Cruikshank passed behind my mother to the sink. "I won't have my son being brainwashed, Fay. I told you this was a bad idea."

"There's no need to overreact. It's entirely harmless."

"Harmless, my ass."

My mother circled the kitchen island. "Please, Artie. He's had such a hard time of it, you know, and—" She'd reached for my stepfather's shoulder, but he shook her off.

"We all have our troubles," said Mr. Cruikshank. "I'm not above sympathy. But I don't need a nut-job straight out of the loony bin messing with my kids."

"They're just children. You shouldn't—"

"They're old enough. They have every right to know the truth. Oren and I are always going to be honest with each other. Right, Oren?"

"Right," Oren agreed.

Mr. Cruikshank stepped over to Oren and me, placing one large, moist hand on each of our shoulders. "Kevin's uncle spent some time in an insane asylum," he said.

"A long time ago," my mother added. "After Aunt Caroline died."

"His head's still soft," said Oren's father.

That appeared to be the final word. Mr. Cruikshank tucked a paper napkin into his collar and began to skim *The Tundra Times*. My mother orbited the table with the salmon platter, scraping fish onto plates; she rounded again with a side dish of corn on the cob. (I knew enough not to taste the main meal until the side dish had been served— one of the many "rules of order" that Oren's father had introduced to our household—so I poked aimlessly at the fish with my fork.) When I looked up, my mother was sobbing.

"I don't want to fight, Artie," she pleaded. "I thought it would be good for him—good for them. Give Kevin and Oren a chance to know what little family they've got left." She shielded her eyes with her hands. "I can't see why you're so hung up about what happened. It's been almost twelve years."

Oren's father folded shut the paper.

"Maybe you could look after them," continued my mother. "You could take them out with you. Teach them to fix things."

"You know I don't like to be tied down." Mr. Cruikshank adjusted his thin-rimmed glasses. "Enough of this. Let's talk about something else."

❧

THAT NIGHT, ALONE WITH OREN in our tiny windowless bedroom, I finally had the courage to ask the question that had been gnawing at me all evening. We slept in adjacent beds, a Santa Claus night lamp between us. Posters and newspaper clippings plastered the walls: Indonesian volcanoes, Hank Aaron & Willie Mays, *Hawaii Five-O*. Over the hamper danced a fluorescent mobile of arctic animals: violet polar bears, chartreuse reindeer, aquamarine walruses. Absolutely everything in the room—except my folding cot and clothes—had once belonged entirely to Oren. He didn't seem to mind the intrusion. If anything, he appeared to welcome the company. I can imagine him thinking of his new stepbrother as his first great experiment, gathering empirical data even as he taught me about hammerhead sharks, which he'd seen with his mother at the San Francisco Aquarium. That was the boy I asked, as he helped me lop the feet off my pajama bottoms, "What's an asylum?"

"It's for crazy people. Where they lock them up."

I let this sink in for a moment. We could hear the television murmuring in the living room. Outside, the wind rattled the siding.

"Do you think Uncle Rex is crazy?" I asked.

"He was in an asylum."

I turned over on my side. "I don't think he's crazy," I said. I watched Oren's shadow, nearly motionless, on the far wall. "I think it *could* be flat."

"Miss Langley says it's round," answered Oren. "Papa says it's round."

Isabel Langley taught a combined second, third, and fourth grade at the Bear Claw Consolidated School. She was young, not un-pretty, popular—though a bit birdlike in a long-necked, pecking sort of way—and Oren was her favorite. (She choked to death on a halibut bone while my stepbrother was in college; he flew back from Fairbanks to read at her funeral.) At one end of Miss Langley's splintering desk stood a plastic clock shaped like an owl, at the other end a somewhat weather-beaten globe. She had a fondness for carrying the globe to the front of the classroom and pointing out distant locations. Chicago. Moscow. Vietnam. Uncle Rex called her pitiably ignorant.

"Maybe Miss Langley's had her brain washed," I said.

The voice that answered was not Oren's, but my mother's. She stood in the door frame, her skin bathed in soft pink light. "Maybe, honey," she said. "But Miss Langley went to school with Oren's father. She's very smart."

My mother entered the room, carrying with her that faint, comforting aroma of lavender. She kissed me on the forehead, as she did every night. Then she wiggled my big toe, lovingly. (Oren insisted he was too old for kissing.)

"Can we go to the library tomorrow?" Oren asked. "Before we go to Uncle Rex's?"

"If you want, honey. More shark books?"

"Nope," said Oren. "Something new."

"Something new," echoed my mother, feigning wonder.

"We may have to order it."

"What might we have to order?"

"The book I want," said Oren, matter-of-factly. "By Cyril of Jerusalem."

℘

I DO NOT WISH TO LEAVE YOU with the wrong impression. Although "scientific" instruction was an important feature of our visits with Uncle Rex, he was far from monomaniacal. (It would be several years, yet, before his arrest for harassing Buzz Aldrin at the Fairbanks airport.) Most of our time together was spent aboard the Boniface's Revenge, exploring the Delta.

One afternoon, we cruised downstream to a cluster of abandoned bungalows that had previously been a school for Moravian teenagers. The church kids had left everything behind—crates of hymnals and German grammars, jugs of Skippy peanut butter, a room full of identical Singer sewing machines. It was something of a local Pompeii, an entire community preserved in amber. A scene from the end of the world. Only in a few smaller cabins, where a weasel had poked its nose through an open door, did the shredded mattresses and scattered chess pieces suggest a more gradual slide into ruin. ("Costs too much to carry this junk back upriver," Uncle Rex explained.) Uncle Rex salvaged a steam iron and a lug wrench from the site. Oren came away with a coyote skull and a *Playboy* centerfold he'd discovered beneath the shelving paper in the superintendent's bureau. I didn't think to take anything.

On the return trip, Uncle Rex jerked the throttle to top speed and, without warning, stepped away from the wheel. "You're captain now, boy," he declared.

We were headed dead-on for a sandbar. I had little choice. Yet when I finally started to get the hang of the wheel—the hydroplane of the straightaways, the hard torque of the turns—Uncle Rex shuffled to the back of the boat and added: "I'm going to pull the plug out now. So don't slow down, boy."

"What happens if he slows down?" Oren asked.

Uncle Rex uncapped a bottle of beer. "We sink."

ℭ

ON ANOTHER OCCASION, Uncle Rex took us hunting for ptarmigan. It was late July, nearly a month before the start of the legal hunting season, which assured us the best grounds for ourselves. Foremost among these was an elevated tract beyond Dead Russian Cove that had once been headquarters to the Bureau of Land Management. A wire-mesh fence ringed the property, black-and-red NO TRESPASSING notices suspended every twenty yards. Two concrete fuel drums flanked the main lodge. Bearflowers and fireweed poked through cracks in the asphalt driveway. Uncle Rex steered us through willow and dwarf birch until we reached a collapsed swath in the fence. On the other side, a ridge of tundra extended to the horizon. The Samoyeds, Antipodes and Capricorn, trotted confidently beside the undergrowth.

All three of us had 12-gauge shotguns. Oren held his diagonally across his chest like a militiaman. I dragged mine behind me in the cottongrass.

"Mid-summer's the best time for these guys," Uncle Rex explained. "They'll eat just about anything if they have to, berries, catkins, but they're really after caterpillars. Makes their mouths water."

"Yuck," I said.

"Now's the best time for caterpillars," Uncle Rex added. "Before they turn into moths."

"Or butterflies," my stepbrother said.

Uncle Rex glanced over his shoulder at Oren. "Take care with that gun," he said.

We cut quickly across the level ground. My arms in my long-sleeved shirt itched from the sweat, but I didn't dare complain. Oren stopped to pee behind a solitary spruce. Uncle Rex kept walking.

"That used to be your dad's gun," Uncle Rex said. "He must've killed a dozen caribou with that thing."

"It's heavy."

"Good. We'll make a man of you yet."

Uncle Rex pointed toward a small rise marked by several dead willows. "Ptarmigan," he said. I saw nothing. Uncle Rex dropped to his knee and fired. "I liked your dad," he said through tight lips. "Straight-shooting guy." He dispatched a second salvo, then a third. A thin wind rippled the meadow. "Helluva lot better than what your mom's got now." (Uncle Rex had already warned us multiple times about not mentioning our off-season shooting to Mr. Cruikshank. Now he added: "Sonovabitch will turn us in for the reward.")

At that moment, Oren charged up the path behind us. He held the gun in front of him, as though it were fixed with a bayonet. To this day, I still don't know whether he heard what Uncle Rex said about his father. "Have *you* ever seen it?" Oren demanded.

"What?" Uncle Rex asked.

"Have *you* ever seen the edge of the earth?"

"More of that, boy? Can't you think for yourself?"

Oren's eyes narrowed. "I *am* thinking for myself."

Uncle Rex strode across the ridge toward the stand of dead willows. The dogs met him halfway, each carrying a limp bird. "Picture perfect," he declared. He tousled both animals affectionately on the tops of their heads. "Your dad and I used to be able to bag a hundred of these guys between us."

"You're ignoring me," Oren persisted. "Have you been there or haven't you?"

"Of course, I've been there," Uncle Rex snapped. His own admission appeared to have surprised him, and he dropped one of the birds. Capricorn dutifully retrieved it, tail wagging.

"No, you haven't."

"You really want to see the edge of the earth? Well, we're going there. Tomorrow morning. Put an end to your nay-saying and namby-pambying once and for all."

Oren let the shotgun fall to his side. He rubbed his tongue over his teeth, as though wiping away a bitter film, and he appeared suddenly unsure of himself. Uncle Rex tossed the second dead bird into his canvas game bag. He'd accidentally picked it up by the wrong end: ptarmigan blood tricked down his wrist to his thumb. A stray feather clung to his jacket like a brooch. The groove between my uncle's eyes grew deeper; the flesh of his cheeks suddenly seemed loose and weary. At seven, I took this expression for disgust. (Now, I recognize it as age—a first slip in confidence, a swift clout of what was to come.) Meanwhile, my own confidence in Uncle Rex soared. It seemed perfectly plausible that my uncle, who knew every last crook and bar in the river, might lead us to the outer bounds of the planet.

Uncle Rex shifted his weight, frowning. Oren slumped down on the tundra with the shotgun balanced over his bare knees. Across the ridge, the ptarmigans settled back into the willow grove. Dozens, possibly hundreds. A phalanx of fowl. All restive and helpless under the white sun.

This was my moment. I did as I'd been told, as Uncle Rex had demonstrated. I dropped to one knee. I looked down the end of the barrel, aiming low. My prize, a plump beige hen, cocked her head. A big, fleshy ball of a target. I released the safety, blocked out the bay of the Samoyeds. As my finger came down on the trigger, the hen suddenly shifted position. So did I.

The recoil knocked me flat-out cold.

∽

OREN'S FATHER DROVE US out to Uncle Rex's the following morning.

It was a damp, unpromising day. The skies were low-slung and overcast. The first breeze of autumn already nipped at our ears. Driving through the town center, past the charred husk that had once been North Pole Hardware, past the shuttered windows of the Happy Chinaman Cab Company, past Huskerman's Outfitting, Zirkowski's Funeral Parlor, past the graveyard of wheel-less, mud-sunk automobiles that flanked Granger's service station, I couldn't help thinking about how far away Anchorage was, how remote Bear Claw lay from the rest of the universe. Our only road, six miles of macadam, looped back on itself. To travel any farther, you needed a boat, or a good set of knee boots, or a booking on the twice-weekly propeller service over the Alaska Range. Our remote little outpost was the perfect base camp for a journey to the planet's edge.

My face looked ghastly. One of my eyes was swollen shut; the other had acquired the raw, bloodless look of a pink onion. Three incisors remained under my pillow, awaiting a delayed visit from the Tooth Fairy. ("Oh, the Tooth Fairy," Oren's father had said, cryptically, in the pickup. "We don't do that.") If my mother had been around, I imagine I'd have awakened seventy-five cents richer—and that our trips to Uncle Rex's would have met a swift end. Yet she was in Tunuak that morning, measuring intraocular pressures with her tonometer. Mr. Cruikshank, while vocally concerned with our intellectual and moral upbringing, took less interest in our physical welfare. ("Children are resilient—like weeds," he quipped.) When Uncle Rex explained how I'd removed the Remington from the gun closet and fired by accident, Oren's father nodded suspiciously, but voiced no doubts. (It's likely he believed Oren responsible for my injuries, that his son had bested me in a battle royal, even that he was secretly proud.)

When Mr. Cruikshank deposited us on the shoulder of the ring road, about a hundred yards below Uncle Rex's cabin, he warned me: "No more accidents. Best heal over before your Mama gets back." (Oren's dad never walked us to Uncle Rex's door. "No time for kid games," he complained. "Got to earn a living.") I was extra conscious of him that

LESSONS IN PLATYGAEANISM

morning, fearing how he'd react if he knew our destination.

We found Uncle Rex seated at the lopsided wooden table in his den. This was the room that housed his vast library and his own original manuscripts. The deep-set shelves also contained Aunt Caroline's heirlooms: traditional *agayu* masks, a raincoat sewn from seal guts, an oar carved by her grandfather. Her own ashes rested in a small grass basket above the fireplace. (My mother would ultimately turn over all of these artifacts, except the ashes, to the Yup'ik cultural center.) On the wooden table, in front of Uncle Rex, sat his mechanical Underwood typewriter. "So you came back," he said, looking up from the keys. "Hold your horses, boys. This letter's to the governor."

"What's it about?" Oren asked.

"School curriculum. Stuff and nonsense."

Uncle Rex looked down at the keys while he typed, pausing periodically to drag on his smoldering pipe. A cloud of blue smoke wafted above our heads. We waited, standing, while his fingers drummed a staccato on the typewriter. After several minutes, he rotated the letter off the roller. "All done, boys," he said, blowing the ink dry. "Ready for some fishing?"

"The edge of the earth," Oren said. "You promised."

Uncle Rex plucked his yachtsman's cap from a wall peg. "We'll get there. Might as well try our luck along the way." He retrieved a large cooler from the refrigerator and led us down the familiar iron stairs.

"Your helm, captain," he said to me. "Down river."

By now, of course, I was an old hand at piloting the johnboat. I took the curves tight, maxed out the throttle whenever possible. And I knew the tricks of the trade: to ride another vessel's wake, to find the deep water along the steeper bank.

"How far down?" I asked.

"As far as you can go."

Uncle Rex passed me an icy beer. "You'll need that, boy," he said. "Keeps you warm." He handed another can to Oren. Then we rode in almost dead silence, for nearly two hours, past the Moravian Church school, the ptarmigan hunting grounds, the turnoff to Dead Russian Cove. The Kuskokwim grew broad and rough—a giant, angry plain. We passed two fishing trawlers, large commercial vessels. Opposite from what was either Tuntutuliak or Saint Christopher's—who could ever tell?—a barge, lumber loaded high on her belly, cruised across our bow. As we sped south, numerous tributaries branched off the river, some nearly as large as the Kuskokwim itself, and several times I lost the channel entirely. When I looked to my uncle for help, he shrugged and pointed. And then, around noon, the channel opened up, and the banks fell away—and suddenly, sublimely, we were out on the naked sea.

The surf picked up, lashing us with spray. I struggled to control the boat. "Cut the engine," Uncle Rex ordered. "Ride the current." I shifted to neutral. We bobbed slowly away from the shore. A patch of golden sun slapped its warmth on the boat.

At that moment, a flock of trumpeter swans—thousands—rose over the ocean. They swooped up from the Delta, wide, silver-winged, and faded into specks at the horizon.

"Pretty amazing, boys."

He stood at the prow, beaming. I smiled, too.

So far, Oren had said nothing. He was sitting on the plastic beer cooler, his arms folded across his chest. "It's not the edge of the earth."

"Out there," said Uncle Rex, pointing. "There's the edge."

Oren sniffled. "The birds wouldn't go over the side." He added, knowingly, "You're lying."

Uncle Rex crumpled his beer can in his fist. "What did you say, boy?"

"I'm not stupid," said Oren. "You're lying."

The crushed can clattered against the floor of the boat.

"You want lying?" Uncle Rex shouted. "I'll show you lying." He stepped past me and took hold of the wheel. "Edge of the earth, here we come."

I was suddenly swamped with terror. I expected Uncle Rex to follow the swans—to send us cascading over the edge. Instead, he spun us toward the Delta. We turned so fast we caught the spray of our own wake. Cold water stung my face, pinned my jacket to my chest. The Boniface's Revenge practically skidded up over the surf. "I'll show you the edge of the earth," Uncle Rex shouted. "You wait and see." The ocean vanished as quickly as it had appeared. We cruised back up the Kuskokwim, tearing water.

Uncle Rex followed a tributary I didn't know, then another. It felt as though we were traveling in circles. I was anxious, but still hopeful. I was afraid to speak. Oren sat motionless, wearing a thin, smug grin across his lips. Without warning, we jolted to a stop beside a flat, grassy bank. Uncle Rex moored the boat on a drift log.

"Out, boys," he commanded. "March."

We preceded him up the shore like prisoners of war.

At first, the ground was even, but soon it acquired a rolling, almost buckled grade. More and more evergreens pushed through the scrub. Finches twittered in the willow branches, bursts of royal purple. Terns circled overhead. Our own boots squeaked on the spongy earth. I was thirsty. I needed to pee. The sun had burned through the clouds, bringing with it mosquitoes and black flies and no-see-ums. I cannot do justice to my relief when we scaled one final rise and emerged at the edge of an embankment. We *had* to stop. The trail ended at a thirty-foot drop. This was a veritable cliff by the standards of western Alaska. At the bottom, green water lapped gently on a muddy beach.

I recognized where we were. The other side of Dead Russian Cove. Uncle Rex had marched us up the far bank of the river.

"It's *still* not the edge of the earth," said Oren.

I stepped a bit closer to the precipice. Out on the water, a small gray boat—not much bigger than our own—floated with the tide. A young couple nuzzled at the stern. Their backs were to us. His was wide, dense. Her neck protruded like a sunflower stalk. I shouted to them, mischievously, just as the current shifted their position. "Ahoy!" I called. Oren's father looked up at us, squinting against the sun. At his side, wearing tinted glasses, sat Isabel Langley.

For a brief moment, the cove went silent: birds, wind, water. Then Mr. Cruikshank cursed loudly into the ether. Miss Langley tried to take his elbow, and he cursed at her as well.

Oren's father pulled anchor. He left behind a sea of ripples, nothing more.

"What do you say, boys?" asked Uncle Rex. "Have we had enough adventure for one day?"

Neither Oren nor I said anything.

"I thought as much," said Uncle Rex.

∾

AFTER THAT, WE DIDN'T STAY at Uncle Rex's again.

The following morning, without any reference to our encounter at Dead Russian Cove, Oren's father drove off in his Dodge pickup. "You're in charge, Oren," he said. "Take care of the house. I'll be back before supper." (Whether he went off to regrout bathtubs and recalibrate carburetors, or to rendezvous with Isabel Langley, I still don't know.) Oren and I stood at the end of the gravel path, watching the vehicle jolt away over potholes. Eventually, Mr. Cruikshank rounded the bend and was gone. That left just the two of us, the windswept yard, the gray Alaskan sky.

Oren leaned against the wooden gate. He'd hooked his thumbs through the belt-loops in his dungarees. "The bottom line is that it's round," he said.

"No," I said. "It's not."

Between my stepbrother and me extended a patch of dry earth, a moonscape of paint-can lids, candy-bar wrappers, rusty nails. Near the fence stood a ramshackle pile of red bricks, the remnants of an unfinished masonry project.

"It's flat," I insisted. "Like plywood."

Oren shook his head. "Face it. Your uncle's a loony."

I think Oren intended to say something else, but I kicked him in the knee. Hard. Then I kicked him again between the legs. He staggered sideways, his eyes wide. When he came back at me, flailing, I clawed at his neck. Eventually, we toppled together into the dirt. Although Oren was substantially bigger than me—I was a decidedly puny seven year old—he'd fallen square on his back. While I punched and scratched from above, the rusty nails jabbed his flesh from below.

"Mercy," Oren finally begged. "I give."

I let up the pressure on his chest. He took small, sharp breaths. Three large scratch marks ran from below his left eye to his chin, and his nose hung sideways, bleeding. Across the street, Mr. Huskerman's German shepherd tugged at her chain.

I sat up, stunned at my own power. Oren leaned forward on his elbows, coughing up bloody phlegm. He glared at me. To my amazement, he added, matter-of-factly, Galilean: "It's still round, you fucker."

That's when I snapped. I lunged onto him again, pinning his arms over his head. Somehow, I got hold of a large square brick and held it inches above his shattered face. "It's flat!" I shouted. "It's flat! Say it! Say it now…!"

"Okay, okay," he pleaded. "It's flat."

I knew it wasn't, of course. I already understood that the planet was large and round and inescapable, but I didn't care. That morning, Uncle Rex was far more important to me than science, or truth, or even the life of my stepbrother. To the end of the earth, I would have defended him—and beyond. •

Bioethics for Dunces

LEONARD KNEW LIFE'S RISKS: He might return home one afternoon to have Corinne tell him that his father had fallen on the stairs and fractured a hip. That his father had fallen from a ladder and fractured his skull. That his parents had driven off the Cormorant Island Bridge and into the sea. He might return home one afternoon, any afternoon, to have Corinne tell him that Lenny Jr. had flunked out of school. That Lenny Jr. had been arrested for smuggling immigrants. That Julie Ann was giving blowjobs to tourists for money. He might return home one afternoon, that afternoon, to find Corinne, his darling Corinne, not even fifty-two, cold to the touch from a brain aneurysm. He might return home to find everything gone—Corinne, Julie Ann, the house—charred to ash in a brush fire. Or he might be accused of a crime he hadn't committed. He might be accused of sexually harassing a student, several students, several male students. He might fry for abducting somebody's little boy. And each year how many members of the faculty, junior members of the faculty, grandparents and ex-spouses and stepchildren of members of the faculty, suffocated in sink holes, or went septic after cat bites, or faded into Parkinsonian dementia?

Leonard knew it would be something. Eventually, inevitably. Yet when the kitchen phone rang one balmy Saturday morning while he was transplanting larkspur seedlings into the back garden, when he watched through the glass as Corinne stopped curling the phone cord around her fingers, as the decades of joy drained from her face and his own body quivered at the horror that had befallen their daughter—he already knew, untold, that it was Julie Ann—from that moment until the morning he and Corinne left the hospital for the final time three hundred sixty-six days later, everything that happened seemed utterly impossible.

ᏚᏏ

THEY HAD DRIVEN TO SARASOTA only once before. That had been in '74, when abortion was just legal, when Tony Ambrosino was the only provider south of New Jersey. Dr. Ambrosino was a self-styled "jack Catholic" who'd lost a girlfriend at a clinic in Puerto Rico, on a makeshift operating table, he added, that had once been a billiard table. The obstetrician had insisted on recounting the whole episode, man-to-man, while Corinne was in post-op; Leonard still used the story—and the image of a Foley catheter that Ambrosino had sketched on the back of an advertising circular—in his "Bioethics for Dunces" seminar. But Leonard had stayed clear of Sarasota ever since, had turned down several offers to deliver medical grand rounds there. Over the years, active avoidance had solidified into habit.

"Can't you drive any faster?" Corinne demanded. Her arms were wrapped in a fetal hug around the canvas bag that contained Julie Ann's toiletries, and she swayed as though to the gentle rhythms of an invisible ship.

Leonard did not answer. He was already hovering between eighty-five and ninety. A perverse part of him—even at this crisis—wanted to get pulled over so that he might have the satisfaction of telling the police that yes, he knew exactly how fast he was going, and wouldn't they do the same if their daughters had been critically injured? But as he played out this scenario in his head, as he imagined arriving at the hospital with an escort, the traffic suddenly slowed him down to fifty, and then twenty. An accident: a flatbed truck had strewn a cargo of bicycles across the asphalt, and a team of state troopers was clearing them one at a time. On their first drive to Sarasota, the old state route had been lined with mutilated combines and shacks of corrugated tin. Now billboards crowded the highway, blaring WILL THE ROAD YOU'RE ON GET YOU TO MY PLACE? —GOD and IF YOU LIVED HERE, YOU'D BE HOME ALREADY.

Corinne broke the silence. "You know what I'm thinking?" She was looking away from him, out the window. "It just didn't feel right for me."

"What?"

He knew what, of course—even after three decades. She had used the exact same phrase, in the present tense, as a sophomore at Southwest Florida. "I'm glad that other women can do it, you know," she'd said as they drove to see Ambrosino. "It just doesn't feel right for me." But she'd done it anyway. He'd convinced her. And when they returned home the following afternoon, they'd heard on the radio that Nixon had resigned, and to Leonard the world had seemed a fundamentally better place.

It didn't surprise Leonard to anticipate his wife's thoughts. This was marriage, after all: being able to pick up threads of a conversation, without context, after thirty years of silence. If Corinne *hadn't* mentioned the abortion, he realized, now *that* would have surprised him.

"I love you," he said, wanting to connect. "Very much."

"Maybe God is punishing us."

"God punishes those who punish themselves," Leonard snapped back—unthinking, as he might have answered a student who invoked theology in class. He immediately wanted the words back. "It will all be okay."

"I love you, too, for what it's worth," said Corinne, squeezing his forearm.

He remembered something else, though, on the way into the hospital parking lot, something that had bored under his skin many years before. Lenny Jr. had been in seventh grade, Julie Ann in fourth. He and Corinne had run for the two open seats on the Cormorant Island School Board. On the candidates' circular, prepared by the Chamber of Commerce, he had listed his religion as secular humanism. Corinne—liberal, free-thinking, Schopenhauer-reading Corinne—had written down Presbyterian. "Hedging my bets," she'd said with a grin.

Against what? he'd always wondered. Until he saw Julie Ann.

∞

THE HOUSE OFFICER IN THE ICU was a lanky South Asian kid named Dr. Prashad who appeared to recognize Leonard's name, but didn't know how to work this fact into the conversation. Leonard empathized. What could Prashad ask? Are you the guy who hosts the medical ethics show on public radio? The guy who interviews the parents of comatose children? The ICU does not lend itself to irony. But the acne-ridden Prashad was a bit too clinical, a bit too impressed with himself for Leonard's tastes. When the resident pulled the curtain around Julie Ann's bed to give the four of them privacy, Leonard felt forcibly quarantined.

"She did a number on herself," Leonard said.

"You might say that," Prashad said. "Ethylene glycol is a potent poison. And we didn't know she had it in her for several hours."

"How *couldn't* you know?" demanded Corinne.

"We thought it was the trauma from the head wound," Prashad explained.

"And it's not every day you have a kid who drinks a bottle of antifreeze *and* jumps off a fourth-story balcony," Leonard said.

Prashad shifted his weight from one leg to the other. "No, it's not."

"So how bad *is* the damage?" Leonard pressed. He was aware that his tone sounded flip, even callous, but he wasn't ready for the alternative. Certainly not in front of Prashad. If anything, he wanted the smug prick to squirm a bit. "Is she cash-and-carry, or will we have to leave her here overnight?"

"I'm afraid it's a bit more serious," Prashad said. He warned Corinne not to hold her daughter's hands—the girl had shattered metacarpals in both—and then launched into a long-winded discourse on creatinine levels and dialysis, vision acuity and flicker-fusion decline, fractures of the ulna and radius and clavicle. The upshot was that Julie Ann's kidneys and eyes were permanently damaged.

"How damaged?" Corinne asked.

"That shouldn't concern you right now," Prashad answered. "I think the brain is our first priority. The CT scan shows some swelling, midline shift and several large lesions. And on the Glasgow Coma Scale, your daughter is at Level 3."

Corinne swallowed hard. "Out of how many?"

"Fifteen is fully conscious."

"It could be worse, right?"

"Of course it could," said Leonard. He did not want Prashad to explain that the scale began at three. "Thank you, doctor," he added— more as an injunction to leave than an expression of gratitude. The resident drew back the curtain halfway.

"Hold on a minute," Corinne interjected. "What does all that mean?"

"It's hard to say yet," Prashad said. "I think you'd better ask Dr. Jessup on Monday."

After Prashad left, they stood on either side of Julie Ann's bed in the hopeless yellow-gray of the ICU and waited. Leonard wanted to touch his daughter, but he feared dislodging the casts and splints that gave form to her body. She seemed so helpless, eyes closed, surrounded by rubber tubing, yet still beautiful, like a mermaid beached on a breakwater. Gauze and bedding hid her breathing. Only the gentle dance of bright lines on the monitors offered assurance that life was still present. How the hell could a girl once so robust that he'd carried her around like a sack of potatoes become so fragile that he couldn't clasp her fingers without doing permanent damage? How had last night suddenly become this morning? Leonard prepared something to say—about calling Lenny Jr., about calling his parents—but stayed silent. And then Prashad was suddenly back with a colossal young woman at his side.

"I'm Miss Kempleman," she said. "The volleyball coach."

Miss Kempleman wore pigtails and gnawed nervously at a gold chain around her neck. She extended a long, trembling arm toward Leonard and offered him a small tan scrap of paper. The page had been folded over in two. Then the failed chaperone stood at the foot of the bed, her eyes pleading: please don't hate me, please don't sue me, please don't destroy my meager little life. Like a servant waiting for dismissal.

"We don't blame you," Leonard soothed. He reached over to pat the woman's shoulder to reassure her, but she was so tall that he accidentally rubbed his fingertips against her breast. They both drew back. Quickly, he opened the note and held it so that Corinne could also read:

MOM & DAD
    IT'S NOT YOUR FAULT. I'M TIRED OF BEING UGLY.
    I LOVE YOU BOTH.
                JULIE ANN

Beneath were printed the name and address of the Lazy Flamingo Motel with the first letter in "Flamingo" styled to look like its aviary namesake.

Prashad, who hadn't been able to see the note, waited for Leonard to look up. "I don't know if this is appropriate," the doctor said. "But I wanted to come back to tell you that I listen to you on the radio."

"God damn," Corinne shouted. "Give me a number, doctor? Are her chances of waking up thirty percent? Ten percent?"

She'd caught the resident off guard. "No, Mrs. Barrett. I wouldn't say they were nearly that high."

∾

DR. JESSUP, THE NEUROLOGIST, put Julie Ann's odds at one in one thousand—and that was of her ever breathing on her own. After that, it was another one in one thousand that she'd regain consciousness. And yet another one in one thousand that she'd be able to interact meaningfully with other people. Jessup appeared to be in his early sixties, a broad-shouldered, rugged-featured physician of the country squire variety, and his deep, sonorous voice recalled the South Florida of Leonard's lost childhood. On his office shelves, beside the *Textbook of Traumatic Brain Injury*, sat conspicuous volumes of *The Complete Works of William Shakespeare* and Xenophon's *Anabasis*. If you had to learn that your teenage daughter's chances were one in a million, thought Leonard, here was the man to tell you.

"If Julie Ann were my daughter," Jessup explained, "I'd try to resign myself to the fact that the likelihood of any significant recovery is exceedingly low."

"But there is hope?" Corinne asked.

"We always have hope. That may be the most redeeming attribute of our species. But in this instance, I'm afraid, the odds are long."

Leonard had a strong sense of exactly how long. He'd devoted his entire adult life to the quandary of the living dead—to Karen Ann Quinlan and to advance directives, and to the moral and legal intricacies of passive euthanasia. He could quote all of the court decisions, all of the medical case studies. He knew that on July 16, 1983, a Milwaukee woman who had suffered severe head trauma in an industrial accident awoke after twenty-two years in a persistently vegetative coma and asked for an aspirin. And he knew all about Harriet McNamara, the UCLA botany professor who'd been out for six years and now served as an undersecretary in the Department of Agriculture. He had them both on videotape for his classes—and dozens of others. Also films of men and women who were leading productive lives without kidneys, without eyes, without arms and legs. Julie Ann might be the next goddamn Helen Keller. But he also knew the rest of it: the daily heartbreak, the financial destitution, the forsaken siblings, the aging couples whose worlds grew increasingly minute as they warded off bedsores and waited for miracles that lurked just beyond the horizon. He foresaw the false promise culled from Julie Ann's every last involuntary twitch.

Leonard stood up. He crossed Jessup's office to the expansive tinted window and examined the world beyond the hospital: a flock of cattle egrets swooped over the parking lot and settled around an idling pickup truck. "What if we don't want to wait?" he asked. He couldn't hear his own voice.

"She's young," Jessup said. "Give her some time. It won't change Julie Ann's prognosis, but it will help you come to terms with whatever you decide."

"And then?"

Jessup propped the tips of his fingers together. They both knew that Leonard had written the state's guidelines for the withdrawal of food and hydration, that he was searching for a spiritual answer, not a procedural one. "And then I offer you all the moral support that one human being can offer another," Jessup said.

"That won't be necessary," Corinne said. Her eyes were raw from sobbing. She spoke with fists clenched, knuckles white. "We've decided to wait this one out."

⁓

SO THEY WAITED. Julie Ann worked her way up to the neurology ward

BIOETHICS FOR DUNCES

and then to a chronic-care facility adjacent to the hospital. She shared a corridor with the worst of the worst: several stroked-out men in their eighties, a Seminole woman suffering from locked-in syndrome, and two brothers in the final stages of Huntington's chorea. The daughter of the Seminole woman dressed her mother in fashionable street clothes early every morning—floral-print blouses, plumed summer hats—so she looked like something straight out of Madame Tussauds. The two brothers never had visitors. Their father had attempted to end their suffering with a sawed-off shotgun several months before Julie Ann's arrival, but he hadn't the courage to pull the trigger. Now the banished old man faced federal weapons charges. These details came from Little Zenobia, the ever-smiling fundamentalist nurse who helped Corinne with Julie Ann's range-of-motion exercises.

Corinne spent seven days each week in Sarasota. She was out the door before Leonard woke up, rarely back before nine or ten at night. She acquired the faraway, haggard look of perennial caregivers. Transferring Julie Ann to Cormorant Island, or even to Fort Myers, might have cut two hours off Corinne's commute—but she insisted on the proximity of a top-notch university hospital. Leonard didn't object too strenuously. Julie Ann had made a vocation of acquiring respiratory infections. Twice the girl's fever spiked over 104. They'd had to shuffle her back to the ICU repeatedly.

Everybody was supportive, in a slightly distant manner that grew increasingly awkward with time. They sent yellow roses, balloons. They visited in small groups: Corinne's colleagues from the library, the varsity volleyball team, Leonard's sister and nephews from Miami. But nobody ever visited twice. Not even Lenny Jr. Not even Leonard's parents. What was the point? And everybody was so hyper-serious. Corinne's brother in San Diego owned a company that manufactured novelty greeting cards ("Congratulations on your workers' comp claim," "Best wishes on your hysterectomy"), and it would have made Leonard's week to get a note that read: "Congratulations on your daughter's failed suicide bid," but all his brother-in-law sent was a soppy "Get Well Soon" card from Hallmark. The underlying problem was that Leonard's situation lacked a governing social convention. Within two months, acquaintances started to avoid him. They couldn't wish him condolences, nor could they wish Julie Ann a speedy recovery, and they couldn't even curse fate or some specific malefactor, as they might have if she had been struck down by lightning or gang-raped by escaped convicts. Yet if they saw Leonard, they felt obliged to acknowledge the tragedy. Ultimately, they arranged not to see him.

Leonard kept up with his work. If he'd had his druthers, he would have deep-sixed the radio show, but with Corinne on leave, they needed the extra cash. Especially with the co-payments, the prescription drugs. His father had urged him to sue—the school district, the volleyball league, the motel—but Leonard refused. There was no need, he said, to divvy up the suffering.

Soon a new breed of acquaintances sought him out. These were the parents of suicides, the spouses of vegetables, the kith and kin of the positively helpless. They attended his lectures and hounded him after class. They pursued him onto the airwaves. He had the Ugandan health minister on to discuss the ethics of Third World drug protocols, but the callers would all want to talk about Julie Ann. A grandmother from Tampa wrote him that her own daughter had fallen from a hotel balcony while posing for a photograph; she enclosed a copy of the picture. A couple from Everglades City sent him the razor blades that their son had used on his wrists.

And then Corinne found religion. Hers wasn't the Bible-thumping, speaking-in-tongues sort of religion that Little Zenobia pitched. She didn't recruit Carmelite nuns to recite novenas in Julie Ann's name. But she woke up Leonard late one Saturday night and announced, "I'm going to church tomorrow," and then squeezed into a world too small for him to enter.

In his isolation, Leonard took up driving. He'd set out for the

BIOETHICS FOR DUNCES

Pelican Bay Mall to buy shaving cream or lightbulbs, and the next thing he'd know it was near dark and he was approaching the outskirts of Orlando. Usually, he thought about Julie Ann: less and less as the six-year-old beauty who'd given him a jar of fireflies to use as a nightlight, more and more as a rangy tomboy who'd suffered beyond the periphery of his gaze. He had questions, and not just the "why" questions that Corinne kept asking. His questions were more like the questions he wished he'd asked his grandfather before he'd died—about the old man's military service, about his years as an oil surveyor. Leonard found himself wondering how Julie Ann had lived her daily life. Did she steal from the SpeedyMart? Did she drive up to the wilderness preserve and make out with boys? How did she feel about abortion and gun control and the battle over the proposed condominium development on Coconut Street? He always thought about Julie Ann in the past tense. Sometimes he discovered himself thinking about Corinne in that way, too. Sometimes he pulled off the highway at a random exit and napped in the parking lot of a chain motel.

He did stuff to fill time. Unhealthy stuff. He chose random motorists on the Interstate and followed them—to office parks, to houseboats, to the airport at Fort Myers. He entered Internet chat rooms and pretended to be a seventeen-year-old girl. When Leonard returned home one evening after a particularly harrowing weekend at the ICU, he found a pair of roseate spoonbills necking on the veranda. Their courtship ritual reminded him of how he and Corinne used to dance at the Great Marlin Roadhouse, and later at Captain Henry's, so he impulsively decided to pick up a prostitute on Martin Luther King Jr. Boulevard in St. Petersburg. Yet somehow he ended up in Gainesville instead, pounding on Lenny Jr.'s door. His son opened it in his boxer shorts. The ends of his hair were dyed green.

"It's over?" asked Lenny Jr., matter-of-factly. "I'll get dressed." He shouted back into the darkness: "Jill! My sister died. I gotta run."

Leonard shook his head. "No. I just wanted to say hi."

JACOB M. APPEL

[85]

"Hell. At four in the morning?" Lenny Jr. ducked his head around a corner and called out: "Scratch that! I'll be up in a minute."

"I'm sorry to interrupt," Leonard apologized.

"Does Mom know you're here?" Lenny Jr. rested his palm on his father's shoulder. "Shit, Dad. You don't show up at someone's house at four in the morning unless someone's dead."

℃

CORINNE INSISTED on a birthday party for Julie Ann. She ordered a chocolate cake in the shape of a volleyball, and since they didn't permit open flames in the chronic-care facility, she had eighteen candles stenciled in frosting. Little Zenobia hung streamers. The nurse sang while she worked, "A Mighty Fortress is Our God" and "Jeanie With the Light Brown Hair," until Leonard said, "Shut up, damn it!" After that, she just looked sad. Leonard's one solace was that he'd prevailed on the size of the party. Corinne had wanted something large, maybe epic, in the social hall downstairs. She'd thought about renting a bus to transport Julie Ann's friends on the volleyball team. Leonard had talked her down to just the immediate family: his parents, Lenny Jr., her sister. At the last minute, she also decided to invite the locked-in Seminole woman as well, and the woman's daughter. But the morning before the party—after several fruitless hours shopping for birthday presents that would remain forever wrapped—Leonard stormed into Julie Ann's room.

"I'm going crazy, Corinne," he shouted. "I tell you I'm going crazy."

"Shhh!" his wife begged. "Your voice. Please."

Leonard lowered his voice. "Take a look at yourself, darling. What do you weigh now? One hundred pounds? Ninety-five? Why are you doing this?"

Corinne was massaging her daughter's wrists. "Do we have to discuss this on her birthday?"

"Tomorrow will be Shrove Tuesday or the half anniversary of the fall or who knows what. It will always be something. So yes, yes, we do have to discuss this on her birthday." Leonard paused to regain both his breath and his train of thought; he sat down backward on an iron chair. "Ask yourself, Corinne: Why are you doing this?"

Corinne folded Julie Ann's hands across the girl's lap. "I don't know." Her voice was tired, not angry. "I don't fucking know. It just feels right."

"Please, darling. Have some faith in me. I've seen this hundreds of times before. It won't turn out different just because it's happening to us."

"I did things your way last time. I want to do things my way this time."

Leonard sensed his ears turn red. "That was thirty years ago."

"So?"

"So I don't see what that has to do with this."

Corinne walked across the room and adjusted the get-well cards atop the television. Then, without warning, she pounded her fist into the center of the chocolate cake. "Who the fuck knows, Len? Maybe nothing. There is a God! There isn't a God! Who-the-fuck-knows?" Corinne turned on the faucet in the bathroom and washed chocolate glop from her fingers. "You're the fucking ethicist. You figure it all out."

"I did. This morning. I was trying to buy her a present for her birthday, and suddenly I realized I was shopping for a dead girl."

"Stop it! Not in front of her!"

"She's dead, Corinne. D-E-A-D. Dead."

"Stop it! She's not dead until we lose hope. Until *I* lose hope."

"And how long will that be?"

Corinne licked pink frosting off her sleeve.

"How long will that be?"

"I don't know," she said. "Does she look dead?"

☙

SEVERAL INQUIRIES AT THE HOSPITAL directed Leonard to the stark, barracks-like structure that housed Tony Ambrosino's downtown clinic. The obstetrician had set up shop between a seafood wholesaler and a drive-thru liquor store; the liquor store also advertising check-cashing services. Four anti-abortion protesters stood across the street from the clinic: two elderly women, a girl in her teens, and a boyish Roman Catholic priest. The girl held a placard that depicted a fetus and a slogan that read: *Abortion doesn't make you unpregnant; it makes you the mother of a dead baby.* The fetus reminded Leonard of the pickled meats at the specialty deli in Fort Myers. All four protesters held their noses pinched shut. At first, Leonard thought they were expressing their moral opprobrium, but when he stepped out of his car, he realized that they were shielding themselves from the offal of the seafood wholesaler. He covered his own nose, then thought the better of it. No need to be mistaken for a wacko. Leonard walked rapidly, breathing through his mouth.

A stunningly attractive young woman with bright blue fingernails sized him up suspiciously through a wall of double-paned glass. Two armed guards stood like granite pillars on either side of the entryway. The air was cool and sterile.

"No, I don't have an appointment," Leonard explained. "Can you tell him Professor Leonard Barrett from the University of Southwest Florida would like a minute of his time?" The woman with the blue nails looked him up and down again. She summoned an older woman with salt-and-pepper hair over the intercom, and Barrett identified himself again. "I have a show on the radio," he ventured. *Talking Law, Talking Medicine.* The two women conferred, and the older one disappeared through a white door. The younger woman asked him to step away from the glass.

"For security," she said.

"Of course. Security."

He retreated to the center of the vestibule. Several awkward

BIOETHICS FOR DUNCES

minutes later, the woman with the blue nails buzzed him in. "Take a seat in the lobby," she said. "You sure don't look like no college professor."

❧

AMBROSINO LED LEONARD into a sunny kitchenette at the back of the building. Breakfast cereal and condiment jars stood on a Formica-topped table; Leonard noted a trap door beneath the window. "This is my escape route," said the physician, rapping his knuckles against the hatch in the floor. "I got a tunnel down there leads all the way to Sarasota Bay, and a motor boat with the engine running. Just in case." Ambrosino spread cream cheese over a toasted bagel and dappled the spread with anchovies. "You can believe that, if you want. The whackjobs out front would. Or you can believe I've got boxes of moldy records from the early eighties down there. Anyway, want some lunch?"

Leonard shook his head. He was amazed by Ambrosino's vigor: the obstetrician had a mane of shaggy white hair, and his skin hung in loose flaps, but still he hit you with the force of a manatee. Leonard was also amazed by Ambrosino's appetite. The doctor polished off the bagel and went to work on a can of sardines.

"You scared the bejeezus out of Brenda," said the obstetrician. "First time in fifteen years that's happened. She came back here white as starch."

"I have that effect," Leonard said.

"Seems so. A Sears nut, she called you. Straight out of the catalog. But all that's neither here nor there. So I keep inviting you up here for ethics grand rounds, Barrett. I'm batting zero. What shakes?"

"You don't remember me, do you?" Leonard asked. And soon he was in the thick of his story, talking not just about 1974 or Julie Ann, but somehow about everything in between. "And then this morning," Leonard concluded, "I was at the Pelican Bay Mall deciding whether a sweater was an appropriate birthday gift—and I suddenly realized that it depended on whether we have an open casket. Totally nuts!" When Leonard finished, Ambrosino looked at his watch.

"I gotta break out the coat hangers soon, Barrett," he said. "I'm not sure what you're asking me to do for you."

"I don't know," answered Leonard, tears welling under his eyes. "You've dealt with lots of teenage girls. Was it normal that she thought she was ugly?"

Ambrosino shrugged. "*Was* she ugly?"

The woman named Brenda poked her head in the door; she looked sternly at Ambrosino, but said nothing. He began to clean around his canines with a toothpick. "I'm not a rabbi or Mormon elder, Barrett," he said. "I'm just your run-of-the-mine jack Catholic abortionist. But let me tell you something. My mother had an aunt who was in your situation. Her son had been hit by a crate down at the wharfs. That was in the Dark Ages, mind you. Back when termination of life support went by a much less pleasant name. And Granny Clara—that's what we called her, Granny Clara—she took care of my cousin Carlo, day and night. She slept on a mattress in his hospital room." Ambrosino crumpled up his sandwich wrappers and stuffed them into a brown paper bag. "My cousin Carlo lived like that thirty-one years."

"Jesus," Leonard said.

"You're right about that," said Ambrosino. "It was all about Jesus. But I'll tell you what it *should* be about, Barrett. It should be about anchovies. Herring. Smoked fish. Or, at least, that's *my* pleasure. *You* take *yours*." The physician placed five plastic syringes on the clean white tabletop. "There's barely enough time for the living these days. You can't waste what little you've got on the unborn or the already dead."

Leonard sat motionless.

"Morphine," Ambrosino said. "Off the black market. Can't be traced."

"I know what it is."

"Take it. Or don't."

Leonard quickly scooped up the syringes. "There wasn't any billiard table in Puerto Rico, was there?" he said.

Ambrosino locked the white cabinet. "Try not to scare Brenda on the way out."

∽

WEEKS EVAPORATED. Months. The stuffed-shirt house officer, Dr. Prashad, was fired for falsifying his laboratory data; the daughter of the locked-in Seminole woman choked to death at a barbecue; Leonard's father fell on the stairs and fractured his hip. In late December, Julie Ann came down with a full-fledged bout of pneumonia. The new ICU resident, a chirpy young woman named Dr. Barnes, put her short-term chances at "decidedly slim." But by mid-January, several antibiotic cocktails and a small miracle had transformed her back into the healthy comatose vegetable of old. Meanwhile, Leonard carried the syringes in the pockets of his windbreaker; if the day was warm, he transferred them to his briefcase. On several occasions, he held the first needle against her forearm—but he could get no further than the father of the Huntington's brothers had done. Leonard would have ordered Julie Ann's feeding tubes out in a second, if Corinne had permitted it. But clandestine injections smacked of the unthinkable. He knew this was superstition, of course. That Julie Ann *was* dead in all but name. He finally made a deal with himself and circled the sixteenth of March in his pocket calendar, then set about counting down the time. A year and a day, he thought. He'd let nature have her chance. It wasn't his fault, he concluded on day three sixty-five, if she chose not to take it.

∽

SO LEONARD DID what Leonard had to do. He got a lucky break when Little Zenobia's sister-in-law invited her on a cruise, yet another when

Corinne took up group therapy. That meant she'd be gone from nine to ten every morning. The other nurses kept a low profile, particularly if Leonard was around. He had a reputation. Even the calendar conspired in his favor: the sixteenth of March, which was a Tuesday throughout the remainder of the known universe, had transmuted into a Monday at the university to compensate for a federal holiday. Since Leonard didn't teach on Mondays, he arrived at the facility at the same time as his wife.

"Sure you won't come?" Corinne asked. "This once?"

"No thanks. I'm anti-social."

His frustration with his wife had decreased drastically since he'd acquired the morphine—since he'd charted a way out.

"Well, at least make yourself useful while I'm gone," she said. "Do you remember the elbow-flexing exercises I showed you? The ones that prevent contraction."

Leonard forced a smile. "I'll have her playing the drums."

"I'll be back at ten," Corinne said. "You know where to find me."

"I know, I know. Send my love."

"The flexing exercises. Both arms. Don't forget."

He listened to Corinne's steps retreat down the corridor. He did not bother to close the door; that might have raised suspicions. The locked-in Seminole woman was sitting across the corridor—sporting the same threadbare gray bathrobe that she'd worn every day for a month—but she was a harmless witness. Leonard rolled up the sleeve of Julie Ann's gown and examined the blue-and-white mesh of his daughter's forearm. Countless scars and bruises already marked the flesh. You could read her skin like a medical chart. Bleep, said the heart monitor. The ventilator answered, Blee—eep, Blee—eep. Somewhere outside the window, someone revved up a lawnmower. "I loved those fireflies," Leonard said. "I let every last one of them go, but I loved them." He turned his back to the petrified Seminole woman and rolled up his daughter's other sleeve. He did not dare look into Julie Ann's face. As he removed the first syringe from his pocket, the lawnmower rose to a crescendo.

"Noooo!" Corinne shouted. Her purse came crashing down against the side of his head. "Get back! Get back!"

Leonard brandished the syringe like a weapon, retreating around the bed. He stumbled into the end table, and a vase shattered on the tile below. "Please, Corinne. Give me a chance to explain."

"Explain?!" She swung the purse again and knocked the syringe from his hand. It rolled under the bed. "You would have killed her! Your own daughter." Corinne threw the purse into his face, and then started pounding and clawing with her hands. "To my dying day," she threatened. "To my goddamn last breath." Her nails sliced down his cheeks. He tried to ward off the blows, but feared he might wound her.

Then the miracle happened: a one in a million. The monitors howled. The bright lines went flat. In trotted lean young doctors in turquoise scrubs. In trotted businesslike nurses carrying charts. One of the nurses counted backward from twenty; two of the doctors climbed onto the bed. Soon a bald attending caught sight of Leonard and Corrine. He ordered them into the hallway. They were standing side by side, both breathless, blood dripping from the open wounds on Leonard's face, when the same hairless physician brought them the news.

Corinne nodded. She looked suddenly relieved. She reached for Leonard's body, and he let her take it, let her hold onto it, but all he could think about was his daughter. About how she'd been alive that morning and wasn't anymore. •

One Wish

ARLY ONE MORNING, while walking his dog on a stretch of pristine and windswept beach, the veterinarian stumbled upon a genie in an ordinary bottle. This genie appeared in the form of a middle-aged black woman. She was tall and trim and dignified. A brightly colored silk stole wrapped around her neck, and large soapstone antelopes dangled from her ears. The fine streaks of gray in her long black hair glimmered like veins of precious ore. If she had not come from a bottle, she might easily have passed for a high-school principal or the organist in a church. All of this surprised the veterinarian. The first forty-three years of his life had been rather placid, maybe even mundane. Certainly nothing to prepare him for finding a genie. Besides, he would have expected a bare-chested buccaneer with one hoop earring and a bandana hugging his shaved scalp. Or possibly a scantily clad harem girl who sprang from an oil lamp.

The genie didn't speak at first. She stood in front of the veterinarian with her arms crossed and jaw clenched. A furrow showed between her eyes. But after she'd held this pose for a brief eternity, sizing him up as though deciding whether to punish a wayward child, her face softened and she said, "You have spared me from the bottle. What is your wish?"

Her voice flowed rich and slow, like sorghum.

The veterinarian smiled and scratched the back of his neck. Strangers made him profoundly uncomfortable. "I'm glad I could help," he said. Then he drew back the leash of his Newfie, Egypt, who'd been nuzzling the genie's stockings, and continued his walk up the beach.

"Wait," the genie cried. "What is your wish?"

All the veterinarian had done was pull a stopper from a bottle, and he'd only done that to prevent Egypt or another animal from accidentally choking on the cork. He was not the sort of man to expect compensation for common decency. "It's quite all right," he said. "I'm sure you would have done the same for me."

The genie wrinkled her nose. "So what is your wish?"

"I really don't want to trouble you. Don't think twice."

"But I must grant you a wish," the genie insisted. "One wish."

"Not three wishes?" the veterinarian asked. He had meant this as a joke—in the bedtime stories he read to his niece at Christmas, genies always offered three wishes—but he had hardly uttered the words when he feared the genie might mistake his humor for haggling. Indeed, the groove in her brow deepened as she made a scolding sound by clicking her tongue.

"One wish. No more, no less."

The veterinarian sensed that protesting further might actually insult the genie, something he wished to avoid.

"So I can wish for anything?" he asked.

"Anything," replied the genie. "Any one thing."

"What sort of anything? World peace, anything. Or a year's supply of Kibbles 'n Bits, anything?"

The genie's chest seemed to expand with contempt. "Anything."

"Okay," the veterinarian said. "Anything."

He picked up the bottle again and carried it to the dune grass at the top of the beach. Several wooden picnic tables were laid out in a clearing, courtesy of the National Seashore. The veterinarian wiped the dew off one of them with his handkerchief and sat down to think. He was accustomed to making life-and-death decisions on a daily basis, prescribing treatment regimens for heartworm and feline AIDS, but larger questions were well beyond his purview. He'd never bought a home or asked a woman to marry him. He'd known he wanted to treat sick animals since his boyhood. Except for college and veterinary school at the state university, he'd never lived anywhere other than Cormorant Island. The truth was that even putting a patient to sleep required a certain resolve that the veterinarian had never possessed, and he always referred his euthanasia cases to a colleague on the mainland. Of all the people in the world to make such a wish, the veterinarian considered himself among the least qualified.

A flock of plover glided low across the sand. A heavyset man jogged his way up the shoreline and passed the picnic tables without so much as a nod. The veterinarian heard a pair of doves cooing in a nearby copse of oak, a mournful counterpoint to the frenzied lapping of spray. He released Egypt from her leash and let the old dog lumber down to the water. The vet's hands were trembling. The genie stood beside the picnic table, her arms crossed, her gaze fixed, making it all the more difficult for him to focus.

A wish. A wish for any one thing. The veterinarian's first thought was of Helena Joy, his assistant at the clinic. She was only twenty-six and did not feel for him the way he felt for her. He could change that, of course, with a wish. But he didn't know if that was right, if love from a bottle was any love worth having. He also thought of his mother, his favorite person in the whole wide world, who had drowned in a ferry accident when he was nineteen. There hadn't even been a gravestone where he could say goodbye. Maybe, thought the vet, he could go back and prevent her from boarding the boat. But what then? How would his world, his history, adjust to the return of his mother? And—maybe this was more important—how could he be sure that his mother wasn't happier where she was? He certainly did not want to bring her dislocation and suffering. Yes, thought the veterinarian, these are selfish wishes.

Next he thought of all the diseased and crippled animals in the world, poor lame setters and arthritic shorthairs; this brought him to the verge of tears. With one wish he could heal all of these unfortunate creatures. But soon he remembered all of the people in the world, the blind and palsied and tormented. How could one possibly choose between the animals and the humans? And then he thought once again of Helena Joy, his love and hope for nearly five years.

He looked up at the genie. "Can I have some time to think this over?" he asked. "Maybe a couple of days?"

The genie's jaw dropped open and then shut quickly. "I must grant you one wish. I will not be free of the bottle until I have done so."

The veterinarian examined the backs of his folded hands. He had no desire to prolong the genie's imprisonment, certainly not after the eons he feared she had passed in the bottle. But he also didn't want to wish hastily. Opportunities such as this one were rare in life, he knew, and he was not the sort of man to squander a windfall.

"I'm sorry," he said, "but I need a few more days."

The genie's eyes widened, and she stepped away, placing the picnic table between herself and the veterinarian. He retrieved the stopper from his pocket and sealed her back in the bottle.

℘

THE VETERINARIAN APPROACHED the morning's discovery in the way he did all other events of personal or national significance. He discussed it with his dog. Egypt was a Landseer Newfoundland, black above, white below. She'd been trained as a rescue dog for the county's water patrol, but one of her front paws had been caught in an outboard motor and permanently mangled. The county had passed her on to the veterinarian when she was two. Now she was twelve. Every day for more than nine years the vet had groomed her gently and walked her the three miles between his rented bungalow and the animal clinic, past the very spot where he'd found the bottle, but he'd also indulged her with meringue-topped custards and marzipan candies and slices of key lime pie, until she'd grown gluttonous and somewhat torpid. To walk three miles required long pauses to regain her wind.

It was during just such a pause—at a bend in the coast, where a stand of driftwood encroached on the water—that the veterinarian broached the subject of the genie. He confided easily in Egypt; she was attentive, but never judgmental. "So what do you make of that?" he asked. "A wish. At my age. Twenty years ago, old gal, that was when I needed wishes."

Egypt perched on her forearms, panting, like a breath-starved sphinx. When the veterinarian spoke, she cocked her ears. Behind her, lobster traps bobbed on the water.

"Don't start in with that 'age is a state of mind' nonsense. Maybe you are only as old as you feel, but I feel old. You know what I mean, don't you, old gal?" He frisked her neck with his hands, felt the soft warmth of her scruff. "Neither of us have any salad days left in us, do we? No? I didn't think so."

The dog flaunted her canines; she'd long ago given up barking.

"So what do you think, old gal? Part of me wants to run to the clinic this very minute with armfuls of lilacs and sweep Helena Joy off her feet. But that would be wrong, wouldn't it? You're right. Not just to her. But to that boy of hers. And I guess to all the poor animals and people I could have helped if I'd been a bit less selfish. You're right. As always." He fished in his jacket pocket for a sugar wafer and let her scoop it from his palm with her tongue. "But I know you could care less about my pipedreams," he said. "So what would you do if you were in my place? What would you do if the genie had granted you one wish?"

The veterinarian trusted Egypt's judgment. He'd taken an English elective in college, but the only moment he remembered was a quotation from Lord Byron about Newfies. "Courage without ferocity," wrote the poet. "And all the virtues of man without his vices." The vet wished there were a way of transferring the wish to his companion.

"What would you do, old gal?" he asked again. "What would you wish for?"

The dog shuddered in response. All of the tension drained from her forelimbs, and she settled with her legs splayed as though weighed down by the gravity of the question.

"You don't want the responsibility either, do you?" the vet said. "Well, come along then."

The animal didn't budge. She pleaded with big black eyes.

"You had your treat. What do you want now? A joke?" The veterinarian often tried out his jokes on the Newfie. "Okay. So this lawyer is cross-examining a dachshund and the opposing lawyer stands up and says, 'I object, Your Honor. The prosecution is intentionally mixing up human years and dog years to confuse the witness.'" The vet waited, letting the punchline sink in. Egypt merely sunk further toward the sand. The vet bent to his knees. "So what's bothering you?"

The dog whimpered. Her entire face convulsed as though someone were twisting off her skin by turning one of her ears. Pain brimmed from her eyes, and a thin stream of slaver dribbled from her open mouth. The vet tried to turn the dog onto her side in order to ease the pressure on her limbs; she responded with a long deep moan. He thought about crying for help, but the beach was deserted. The clinic was his best bet. Somehow he found the strength to lift the animal and to carry her forward across the sand.

"C'mon," he begged. "Hang in there. Just a few more minutes."

He measured the distance, landmark by landmark. The umbrella-shaded tables outside the Imperial Flamingo. The remnants of an old fishing pier. A coconut palm shaped like a giraffe. The dog felt warm and listless in his arms. At one point, he wondered if this weren't some sort of test, a trick to see if he'd squander his wish on Egypt's recovery. He thought about doing that. All he had to do was uncork the bottle and she might be rejuvenated. But he held back. She'd recover on her own, he thought. She had to. The vet charged up the narrow beach access ramp, frightening an elderly couple from his path. When he finally crossed Great Conch Street—against traffic—and pounded on the door to the clinic with his shoulder, his eyes were misty, and he was cursing under his breath.

Helena Joy opened the door. The veterinarian stumbled past her and deposited Egypt's body onto the examination table in the surgery. The animal moaned again. She curled herself into a loose shell, her paws tucked under her trunk, one haunch raised and quivering. The vet pulled a stool beside the table and sat down beside the patient. He rested a hand on her nape.

"It must be a vestibular attack," the vet said. "It'll pass."

"Are you sure it isn't a stroke?" Helena Joy asked.

It was a stroke, of course. There could be no doubt of that. But a vestibular attack promised recovery, not a shot of sodium pentobarbital.

"A stroke," the vet murmured. "It could be."

"Why don't you sit down and let me do it, doctor," Helena Joy said. "We really don't have any choice."

She wrapped her hand around the vet's wrist and steered him to the sofa in the adjacent room. This was where the patients' owners usually sat. A glass divider offered them a window into the operating room.

The vet watched as Helena Joy hooked up the IV and measured out the lethal dose of barbiturate. She performed the procedure seamlessly, as well as a trained DVM. Egypt's eyes remained open. The only sign of death was a faint odor of incontinence. Helena Joy felt for the animal's heartbeat, then closed her eyes.

The vet reached into his pocket. He explored the smooth glass of the bottle. Soon Helena Joy emerged from the kitchenette with two cups of tea.

"I told Gladys to cancel all of your morning appointments," she said. "Here, drink this."

He took the teacup. "Thank you."

"I'm so terribly sorry," Helena Joy said. "I know how much you loved her."

"She was a dear old gal," said the vet. He wiped his eyes. "It's not fair."

He removed the bottle from his pocket and held it in his lap. It felt as heavy as a millstone. The veterinarian thought about how efficiently his assistant had handled the crisis, how she'd done what he'd been too weak to do. She'd saved Egypt many hours of suffering. This inner confidence was what the vet loved most about Helena Joy.

"Tell me, Helena, what would you do if you were granted a wish by a genie. What one thing would you change about the world?"

Helena Joy sipped her tea. "I'd wish that no harm comes to Simon Peter." Simon Peter was Helena Joy's fiancé, who was now in the Navy, fighting in the faraway war. "That's what I'd wish."

"You sound so sure."

"I am sure. I've thought about it many times. I wouldn't wish for him to come home to me immediately, although of course I want that, because then some other girl's fiancé might get injured in his place. Or, God forbid, killed. But I'd wish he could stay safe until the war ends."

The veterinarian reflected upon this wish. It was both selfish and unselfish. Most of all, it was perfectly reasonable. Simon Peter's pet rabbit had been one of the vet's patients, when the fiancé was a child, and although it unnerved the vet to think of the boy as his romantic rival, he certainly didn't wish him any harm.

"What would you do, doctor," asked Helena Joy, "with a wish?"

"I don't know yet," said the vet. Even as he said the words, he returned the bottle to his jacket pocket.

He sobbed through the night and into the morning, thinking of Egypt, the chaos of her Sunday baths, and her penchant for dead songbirds, and how she frequently stole sandals and thongs from the poolsides of the nearby motels. But he did not reach for the bottle again.

THE VETERINARIAN CONTINUED to walk to work every morning. He passed the isolated stretch of beach where he'd found the bottle, the stand of driftwood beside which Egypt had collapsed, the sheltered cove from which he'd let her ashes drift out to sea. The three miles; once a hop, skip, and jump from the clinic, now seemed a hopeless distance. The vet walked with his head bowed, pausing to prod knots of seaweed with a jagged wooden stick. He did not stumble upon another genie. He did encounter waterlogged tennis balls and abandoned Frisbees, a leather boot missing its sole, the corpses of gulls, countless reminders of his departed companion. Helena Joy suggested that he adopt a puppy. The vet knew that wasn't what he needed.

Egypt's death revealed to the vet how deeply he longed to connect with another human being. It was the great truth of his life. He had much to share, but nobody to share it with. The last person to whom he had unburdened his innermost thoughts was his mother. During his first year at Gainesville, he had visited her on the second and fourth weekends of each month. It was with her that he first shared his secret dream: a nationwide chain of free animal clinics. He spent almost all of his daylight hours thinking of the project—to be paid for by a surcharge on kennel club registrants, a form of national health insurance for pets—and the nervous excitement kept him awake at night. But then came the sinking of the Cormorant Island ferry. When his mother drowned, she carried his grand aspirations with her to the bottom of the Gulf. All at once he was alone. The next years—maybe until he adopted Egypt—were devoted to recovery.

Since his mother's death, the veterinarian had reached out only once. That had been to Helena Joy, maybe two years after she'd come to work with him. At first, he hadn't been too keen on hiring a woman. It wasn't that he'd doubted her competence—many of the best students at the veterinary school had been women—but he suspected that a woman was more likely to get married and quit. Or to have a baby. He did not want to have to hire another assistant in six months' time. He was also somewhat uncomfortable around women, particularly young attractive ones like Helena Joy. But she had been his sister's biology student at the high school. She also came highly recommended; her previous employer, who had retired, wrote in his letter of reference that she would have made a fine veterinary doctor in her own right. But the girl had tipped the scales by bringing with her to the interview an injured squirrel she'd picked up on Sand Dollar Boulevard. The vet would never forget her standing on the porch in her blood-spattered dress—like Jackie Kennedy after the assassination—and asking him to help her bandage the wounded animal.

The vet hired Helena Joy on the spot. She moved into the vacant garret above the clinic. While at first their interactions had been limited to professional matters—terse exchanges regarding dosage and scheduling—the girl's natural warmth soon melted the ice between them. She spoke of her hobbies, which were strikingly simple. She collected stuffed marsupials. She watched nature shows on television. She was writing a children's book about a lonely old opossum who is befriended by a homesick kangaroo. One day, Helena Joy told the vet why she'd become a veterinary assistant: when she was nine, she'd had a puppy named Koala. He was part beagle, part hound, the overflow of a neighbor's litter. Her father discovered that she'd shoplifted several cloth dog toys from the pet-supply shop in Pelican Bay. Rather than punish her directly, said Helena Joy, he had drowned the dog. The veterinarian's assistant wiped back tears as she recalled the episode—the two of them were taking a quick lunch break in the kitchenette—and the vet was struck with an overwhelming urge to hug her in his arms. But he dared not.

For nearly a year, the vet struggled to find the courage to follow his assistant up to her garret apartment, to unburden his feelings, but he did not have it in him. Instead, he wrote her a note. A short, straightforward missive sent through the mail. Days passed, but Helena Joy made no reference to the letter. Her attitude toward him didn't change. The veterinarian began to fear that his confession had been lost, then to hope that it had been lost. What kind of fool was he, after all, to think that a beautiful young woman might fall for a middle-aged old sock like him? Thank God it had been lost! But one Saturday afternoon he received a small tan envelope in his postbox. His heart leapt with joy. Why take the time to write, after all, if the answer was no? It still took him four days to open the letter. Inside, he discovered two handwritten pages, the kindest and sweetest rejection he could possibly envision. The two of them never mentioned the exchange of letters to each other. About a year later, Helena Joy was engaged to Simon Peter—she was almost apologetic when she told him the news—and then the boy went off to the war. Everything appeared settled. That was, of course, before the vet discovered the genie in the bottle.

Now the veterinarian thought about Helena Joy with increasing frequency. What he had once dismissed as impossible could be his for a mere wish. He thought about how much he longed to sit with Helena Joy on the windswept beach, side by side, listening to the break of the surf. He thought about how wonderful it would be to come home from work each evening and to kiss her on her small sharp nose and on each of her baby-fat cheeks. He thought about how he was only one wish away from nuzzling his face in her silky black hair. But he also thought of the boy he would defraud, the young sailor whose heart he would break. And he thought about how hard it would be to face his love, knowing he had won her deceitfully. His mind swirled with the tradeoffs to be considered: abandoned pets he might rescue from death row, orphaned children whose parents he could resuscitate. Some options he did not entertain. Giving the bottle to a world leader or the United Nations, for example. He did not trust men of power. His experience had been that they could do enough damage without his help. Nor did he ask why he, of all people, had stumbled upon the genie. That was like asking why his mother, of all people, had died on the ferry. But even confined to the limited question of whether to wish for Helena Joy's love, his brain whirred helplessly.

Often, the veterinarian spoke to inanimate objects. He would stand before a fire hydrant or a rusting wheelbarrow and ask, "What would you wish for?" "Oh, is that so?" he might answer. "A few dabs of oil." "A new coat of paint." Sometimes he even fulfilled these imagined wishes, pruning overgrown trees, replacing planks in the boardwalk, scrubbing the sinks at the shellfish-washing hut behind the neighboring motel. That kept him busy. But much of the time, when he wasn't seeing patients, he sat on the breakwater behind his bungalow, holding the bottle. Mostly, he just stared at the milky glass and let his mind go blank. He did not remove the stopper. There were few things he dreaded more than having to confront the genie before he was ready to formulate his wish. Once, he lost his balance and nearly dropped the magic vessel into the sea. Another time—nearly two weeks after Egypt's death—he plucked the cork from the bottle without thinking.

The genie rose before him like the statue of some exotic deity. She was wearing a broad-brimmed turquoise hat tufted with a peacock plume. An ivory parrot-shaped brooch graced her lapel. The veterinarian thought she was several inches taller than she'd been before. "What is your wish?" she asked. He sensed a tinge of irritation in her voice.

"I'm not ready yet," the vet stammered. "I'm sorry."

"What, then?"

"It was an accident. I didn't mean to call you."

"Well," the genie said. But she said the word in such a way as to indicate that his behavior was excessively unreasonable. Nearby, a small horseshoe crab inched its way along the concrete parapet of the breakwater.

"Actually, I do have a question," the vet said. "Can I ask for two things if I phrase them as one thing? Do you understand what I mean? Could I ask you to cure all of the sick animals and all of the sick people?"

The genie raised her arm and for a second he feared she would strike him, but she merely adjusted her hat. "One wish," she said wearily. "Only one wish."

The veterinarian took this for a "No."

"What do most people wish for?"

"There are no 'most people.'" She emphasized every word individually, as though speaking to a foreigner or a fool. "There is only you."

"Okay, okay. Don't pressure me."

The genie shook her head. "If you aren't going to make a wish, would you please have the decency to throw the bottle back on the beach where somebody else might find it?"

"Soon," the vet said. "I promise."

❧

THAT EVENING, the veterinarian narrowed down his list of wishes. He sat in the alcove of garden behind his bungalow where the new buds of bougainvillea and canna reached heavenward like the precious hands of supplicant children. On his knee rested a yellow legal pad upon which he'd enumerated nearly three dozen potential miracles. In his other hand, he held a red magic marker. Hour after hour, as the sun descended toward the ocean's edge, he crossed items off the list. Once he'd taken his niece to adopt a dog from a shelter, and each animal they rejected—each animal they doomed to extermination—took months of happiness from the veterinarian's life. Eliminating wishes was far worse. And he thought of more possible wishes as he went along, dreams of speaking the language of dogs and preserving forever the beauty of Cormorant Island. He finally pared his choices down to two. One was the nationwide chain of free animal clinics. The other was Helena Joy. Between these two visions—one giving, one selfish—he remained unable to decide. If only there were someone to ask, he thought. But there was nobody to ask.

The veterinarian arrived at work the next morning in a state of paralytic indecision.

He found Helena Joy already at work in the surgery. Her arms were elbow deep in a portable bathtub filled with tomato paste. There were also dabs of orange sauce on her neck and above one of her eyes. Helena Joy was struggling to dunk a wiry gray cat into the tub, but the animal flailed wildly in resistance.

"She's a stray. I found her out back by the utility shed. The poor baby had been sprayed by a skunk."

"How is she otherwise?"

"She looks okay, doctor. Just hungry and frightened. All she really needs is a good flea shampoo and some old-fashioned TLC." Helena Joy kissed the cat on the top of her forehead. "Oh, and she's pregnant."

"I see. So what are we going to do with the litter?"

"I'm going to keep them," said Helena Joy. "All of them. They'll keep me company, and it will give me something to write about to my grandmother."

Whenever Helena Joy spoke of writing letters, she spoke only of her grandmother. Never of Simon Peter. The vet knew she did this to avoid wounding his own feelings, but it only managed to make him feel as though she didn't trust him.

"It'll be exciting for your boy when he comes home," the vet said.

Helena Joy glowed. "That, too," she said.

❧

THE FRONT BUZZER went off unexpectedly. Two military men stood on the front porch. One was rigid and stocky like a bull terrier; the other, a meager fellow with a salt-and-pepper mustache, reminded the veterinarian of a schnauzer. At first, the vet assumed that they'd come from the Navy base in Culvert Junction. He held a good reputation among the officers, and he'd treated many a fleet mascot over the years.

But there was too much spit-and-polish about these visitors. They wore seven gold embroidered bars between them. The veterinarian knew that nobody sent a lieutenant commander and a captain out at seven-thirty in the morning over a sick pet. When they asked for Helena Joy, his own body began to quiver.

He watched through the glass divider as the two officers did their duty. Helena Joy sat stiff-backed on the lip of the sofa, her hands folded in her lap, her face as expressionless as a plaster death mask. Tears dribbled down her cheeks; she made no effort to brush them away. Smears of tomato paste ringed her elbows and clumped in her hair. The visit lasted nearly an hour. First one officer spoke, then the other. The veterinarian instructed Gladys to cancel the morning's appointments. Then he sent her home. He would want to be alone with Helena Joy when the schnauzer and the bull terrier departed.

The lieutenant commander fingered his mustache while he spoke; when he finished, he handed Helena Joy a small bundle and a folded American flag. Both officers nodded politely in his direction as they helped themselves out.

Helena Joy remained motionless on the sofa. All of the confidence had flushed out of her face, and her skin looked ashen and haunted. The vet knew this look. It was the same one he'd worn for years after his mother drowned on the ferry. Only now, he had the power to wipe the anguish from Helena Joy's face, to transform her love for the boy into love for himself. All it would cost was a wish. It seemed so obvious, so easy. He went to the foyer closet to retrieve the bottle from the pocket of his jacket.

He heard Helena Joy close the door of the waiting room. "I'm sorry, doctor," she said, calm, almost-entranced, "but I need to go upstairs. I need to."

"Wait," the veterinarian said. "Just one minute."

He reached into the dark closet for the bottle. He'd left it in the far pocket; the air in the closet was heavy with the scent of old wool and mothballs. "Give me one second," he said. "Please."

His hand closed around the smooth cold glass. When he turned to face Helena Joy, she was leaning against the front door with her hand braced on the knob for balance. The vet embraced the cork between his fingers.

"At sea," Helena Joy murmured. "Just drifted away."

The vet's body jolted. "What?"

"He fell off something. Or got thrown off something. I don't know." Helena Joy began waving her arms hysterically. "But he drowned. Simon Peter drowned. SIMON PETER DROWNED!" She stopped shouting and slid down the wall to the floor.

The veterinarian instantly thought of his mother, of the ferry, of the years he'd suffered without so much as a tombstone to mark his loss. And then he remembered the boy, the mere child who'd come to him sobbing over a sick rabbit. It all came upon him at once. He watched Helena Joy grieving on the carpet, her hands around her knees, shaking silently for the graveless sailor. He thought of how lonely he had been, of how long he had waited for this moment. He had to act now, he knew, while still swept up in emotion.

"Helena Joy, my love," he said. "It'll all be okay. Better than okay. I promise."

She looked up. Her eyes were confused, expectant.

The veterinarian closed his own eyes, thinking already of the loneliness to come, of the young Newfie he might adopt from the shelter. But that was what had to be, he thought, and then he handed Helena Joy the bottle. •

Toward Uncharted Waters

T HEY HAD REACHED THAT AGE when couples worry about their grown children, about co-signing mortgages and accommodating in-laws, but the Gayles didn't have any children. They'd never decided against kids—weighty subjects made them both tense—so much as the opportunity had blown in on a fair wind and then drifted out to sea. They'd been compensated with other prospects. Walter had started out a research assistant at the National Weather Service and ended up a forecaster on a major news network. Marcy's field studies for the Washington Zoo had taken them to Kenya and to Madagascar, and three times to the Ituri region of Zaire, where she studied that pathologically diffident quasi-giraffe, the okapi. To celebrate these accomplishments, and their fiftieth birthdays, and maybe also because they would never need to scrimp for weddings or college tuitions, Marcy arranged a sabbatical, and Walter wheedled a full-year leave of absence from the network, and the two of them rented out their garden apartment, sinking the proceeds and most of their savings into a sixty-five-foot used houseboat. Their itinerary was ambitious: the Alexander Archipelago via Tierra del Fuego, with pit stops on the Galapagos Islands and at Lake Nicaragua.

The previous owners had christened the vessel Eleanor. Walter insisted on calling her the Eleanor Roosevelt, because she was both exceptionally sturdy and hideously unattractive. The front of her hull was painted a rich orange that trailed off toward pale yellow at the stern, conveying the appearance of a giant candy corn adrift on its side, and a series of annexes had been appended haphazardly to the deckhouse. The Gayles found her at her moorings in Pelican Bay, Florida. A smaller houseboat shaped like a Dutch windmill was docked thirty yards to their right; the berth at their left sat empty. An Interstate ran parallel to the harbor, and from their deck, Walter and Marcy could see an elevated billboard urging motorists to PLEASE HELP SEND THE PELICAN BAY WOMEN'S SOCCER TEAM TO BARCELONA. At first, the sign provided a source of amusement, but later, as the days drifted into weeks and the necessary repairs to the craft's engine remained incomplete, the essential parts still on order from Mississippi, the billboard came to epitomize their inertia. Marcy relaxed on a chaise longue and hunted shorebirds with her binoculars. Walter fished for snapper off the prow. He purchased a safari suit and grew his whiskers into mutton chops, so that he could have passed muster with Henry Morton Stanley or Sir Harry Johnston.

"They'll be asking us to help them *come back* from Barcelona if those manifolds don't get here soon," Walter complained. His real concern, of course, was hurricane season. It was already late July. Who knew if the Eleanor Roosevelt could handle the blustery surf of early September?

One evening, for a change of pace, they went out for dinner at the Conch & Bull Steakhouse. On the way home, as an indulgence, they stopped for ice cream sodas at Rita's House of Yogurt. The dessert shop was crowded. Ceiling fans whirred overhead, and large black flies droned around the garbage bins. A teenage couple entered behind the Gayles, the boy muscular, the girl square-jawed, both fidgety, and then, without warning, the boy wrapped his elbow around Marcy's throat and held a handgun to her temple. "Empty the fucking register!" he shouted

TOWARD UNCHARTED WATERS

at the cashier. "Fucking now!"

At first nobody did anything. Then Rita heaped handful after handful of currency into the girl's knapsack, while Walter watched his wife, mute and helpless. Moments later, the girl retreated through the swinging screen doors, and the boy, with Marcy in tow, started to follow, his back to the doors, the handgun still leveled at her forehead. At the last minute, he lowered the weapon, then, with the other thick arm, wrenched upward and broke Marcy's neck.

❧

WALTER PASSED ALL OF HIS WAKING HOURS at the hospital. Marcy's prognosis deteriorated to grim and unrelenting. C-4 quadriplegia: She would not walk; she would not move; she would not feel. She would sit forever still like a potted plant. A neurology resident sporting a bola tie spoke rapidly about hyperesthesias and paresthesias, about urinary incontinence and fecal incontinence and the importance of checking extremities for ulcers and lesions, until Walter threatened to throw him over the balcony onto the concrete plaza below. After that, the physicians left them pretty much alone. During the day, Walter sat beside Marcy's bed and tried to convey optimism. He'd say, "It'll all be okay, I'm sure," and he'd pat her on the knee, or the shoulder, but she couldn't feel his touch. At night, he'd pace the deck of the Eleanor Roosevelt, clutching the rumpled map of their aborted voyage, and think of the places they would now never visit, of the eternity his wife would live trapped in a shell. She might live another thirty, forty years—forty years without brushing her own teeth or controlling her own bladder. But what amazed Walter most was how rapidly life continued around him. The police apprehended the teenagers, but they were only thirteen and pleaded guilty to juvenile offenses. The missing manifolds arrived for the engine. The Emerald City, a chrome-green vessel sporting a bright red horse for a figurehead, docked at the empty berth beside their own.

And one torrid afternoon in mid-August, Walter wheeled Marcy up the gangway and onto the deck of their temporary home.

"How do you like that?" Marcy said. "They changed the billboard."

Walter looked up at the opposing embankment. The new billboard read KEEP USING MY NAME IN VAIN AND I'LL MAKE RUSH HOUR LONGER. —GOD

"I don't like it at all," said Walter.

"Do you think they made it?" Marcy asked.

"Do I think who made what?"

"The girls. Do you think they made it to Barcelona?"

"They must have."

"Not necessarily," Marcy said. "They might have given up. Some people do give up, you know."

Walter did not answer. He rolled Marcy into the shade, squeaking the wheels along the deck, sending a cormorant gliding across the turquoise bay. They had ordered a special chair that Marcy would be able to control by blowing into a plastic tube, but it wasn't to arrive for several weeks. What a strange thing, Walter thought, to look forward to. Yet when he and Marcy spoke of the future, it was always of such minor things: could they afford to install a mechanical lift in the boat? Had they arranged to extend their stay with the harbormaster? Was it possible for Marcy to collect disability compensation during her sabbatical? Of the past, they didn't speak at all. Marcy had once taught Walter a peculiar superstition surrounding the okapi, a turn-of-the-century zoologists' taboo against discussing or even naming the creature in its presence, and now a similar prohibition hung over his wife's injuries, over the entire twenty-six years of their marriage. All of their conversations felt formulaic, as scripted as broadcasting the weather. Walter recalled the one time he'd deviated from that script, thanking a particular local politician on the air for three straight days of high ozone levels and apologizing, hat in hand, the next evening after a blitz of irate phone calls, but even that episode he dared not mention. The Gayles had arrived independently at a tacit understanding: their only hope lay in living day by day.

Walter and Marcy quickly acquired the habits of retired couples. Some mornings, they played backgammon or anagrams or filled out the crossword puzzle in *The Miami Herald*; other mornings, Walter read to his wife from the collected correspondence of Mungo Park. This imposed inactivity exhausted Marcy quickly, and she passed most afternoons dozing or gazing hazily at the tourist resorts across the inlet. Walter struggled to remain active, to keep up his hourly recordings of wind speed and barometric pressure, but within days he had contracted Marcy's lethargy. Soon, casting a fishing line over the side took an effort. What little energy he did have was devoted to his wife's comfort: dabbing the sweat from her upper lip, brushing the bangs out of her eyes. At nightfall, he carried her limp, fragile body down into the cabin and placed it gently on their soft double bed. This act gave him that queer discomfort he always experienced when entrusted with another's prized possession, such as when his grand-aunt once asked him to transport a box of antique porcelain to her new apartment, a fear that one misstep on his part might destroy something precious and forever irreplaceable. Walter knew another husband might carry Marcy's body to the side of the boat and gently set her adrift upon the blanket of aquamarine sea, but he would never do this. He couldn't. So every night he woke up at twelve and again at three to turn over his wife's body, to prevent the ulcers and lesions and bedsores that might lead to infection, and every night he wept at the sight of her small gentle face sunk into repose on the pillow.

One night, Walter woke to find Marcy shivering. For a moment, he thought she'd regained sensation—quadriplegics, he recalled, don't shiver—but it was just the quaking in her neck undulating along the bed sheets. The dim light gleaned grotesque horror from her eyes. "It's okay now, dear," Walter soothed. "What's wrong?"

"I was afraid that...." Marcy said. "You're not going to kill me, are you? I know that sounds crazy, but I just had this horrid vision you might think I wanted that. But I don't. I don't. I'm too scared to want that."

Walter pressed his hand to her cheek. "I love you," he said.

"I know that. I was afraid you might do it *because* you loved me. And if you tried, you know, I wouldn't be able to stop you."

A thunderous explosion stifled Walter's answer. He tumbled forward onto Marcy, crushing her ribs, as a second and a third blast sent glassware toppling off the end tables. Torpedoes? A burst boiler? Walter sliced open his hand on the wardrobe as he struggled into his dressing gown.

"Stay here!" he shouted at Marcy instinctively. "You know what I mean," he added. His head scraping the door frame above the narrow stairway, Walter climbed onto the exposed deck with his brow throbbing and blood pooling between his fingers. He pressed his injured hand into the folds of his robe and gained his bearings among the coconut palms, the harbor shadows, and the flickering buoys out on the lagoon. The bite of the damp night air quickened his senses.

He sighted the commotion on the deck of The Emerald City. A vapor of smoke hung in the air above four vintage cannon that several of the revelers had apparently just discharged toward a nearby beacon. Other partygoers were waltzing to a silent band, some decked out in pointed hats and party favors. One woman disguised as a giant rabbit, another as Marie Antoinette with a blood-soaked guillotine for a collar, a number of the men staggering arm-in-arm in what appeared to be an imitation goose step. A banner draped from the side of the deckhouse read HAPPY BIRTHDAY, LEON TROTSKY! in golden letters on a red background. A hammer and sickle marred the corner of the standard. All of the revelers were a full generation younger than Walter. One of them, a tall man of about thirty, sporting a striking orange beard, appeared to be in charge of the festivities.

"Enough with the artillery," the bearded man ordered. "We have neighbors!"

TOWARD UNCHARTED WATERS

"Praise the neighbors," a voice shouted from the deckhouse roof, "and pass the ammunition!"

Another voice said: "It's always those bourgeois neighbors who kill the revolution."

"I'm serious," the bearded man said again. "It's my fucking boat. And I'm serious."

An uncomfortable hush washed across the party. A blonde woman in her twenties wearing Mardi Gras beads and a bikini top grabbed the bearded man by the hands. "Let's play cyclone," she said. "C'mon, Reggie. Let's have fun. Let's play cyclone." The girl rocked forward, kissing him on the lips, then swung outward and allowed him to twirl her in circles. The revelers cleared away space for the spinning couple. "Faster!" the girl shouted. "Faster!" The bearded man released one of her hands. For a split-second, Walter feared he might release the other as well, launching the young woman in the direction of the Eleanor Roosevelt, but instead he lifted the girl off the ground and held her stationary above his head. The audience broke into applause. Walter watched through his binoculars.

The bearded men carried the girl, still above his head, to the railing. "It's my turn to choose the game," he said. "How about we play flood?" He made as though to toss the girl into the water.

"Hurricane!" Marie Antoinette called out.

"Tidal wave!"

"Monsoon!"

Through all of this, Walter feared for the girl's safety, but then he trained his lenses on her sharp perky face and observed that she was giggling. The red light from hanging paper lanterns reflected off her earrings. "Coward!" she mocked through her laughter. "Stinking coward!" The bearded man's arms stiffened at the elbows, and he catapulted the girl into the opaque water.

The young woman's splashing shattered Walter's trance. The bearded man quickly extended a pole to the girl. Walter waited until he'd seen several of the revelers grab hold of the sopping, laughing mermaid-like form, before he descended into the cabin. He despised and envied the giddy young couple on the neighboring boat. He wasn't in the state of mind to confront them. What Walter really wanted to do was to hug Marcy, to assure her that he'd never considered ending her life, but she'd faded into sleep while he'd been out on the deck. This upset him. Something else bothered him, too, something utterly petty and irrational that crept into his consciousness while he lulled on the brink of sleep: The bearded man and his girlfriend had been twirling clockwise; in the Northern Hemisphere, that was the wrong direction for a cyclone.

ℛ

WALTER INTENDED TO SPEAK to the owner of The Emerald City the following morning. He fed Marcy her breakfast of mashed sardines on rye toast, then shaved off his muttonchops and looped a tie around his neck. He wanted his neighbors to know he meant business.

"It's one thing to have a party now and then," he said to Marcy. "Anybody's entitled to a party now and then. I don't begrudge them that. But it's another thing to have to live next door to John-Paul-goddamn-Jones. You don't think I'm overreacting, do you?"

"It was dreadfully loud, dear," Marcy said. "Dreadfully loud."

But The Emerald City was now quiet. Walter searched through the field glasses for some additional offense, for hungover guests or stockpiled explosives, but there wasn't anything to help him work his hackles up. Someone had swabbed down the deck and covered the cannons with tarps. Only the red paper lanterns and a handful of baby-blue streamers remained of the revelry. Otherwise, the vessel was spic-and-span; the railings even sparkled. Walter decided he'd make his move at the first sign of life on the other vessel. Then the harbor patrol arrived—two armed ensigns who Walter thought much too young to brandish weapons—

and the blonde girl led them below deck. Walter presumed the officers would steal his thunder. This seemed terribly unfair—he was the one who'd lost sleep.

Walter walked around to the far side of the Eleanor Roosevelt. A cold front had passed through in the early morning, and the air was crisp and dry. The scent of eggs frying drifted in on the breeze. Walter scanned the shoreline for pedestrians and then unzipped his fly. He let forth a long arc of urine. After that, he watched the turkey buzzards perched on the goddamned blasphemy billboard and condemned both raptors and sign with an acute burst of profanity. When he came back around the wheelhouse, the blonde woman was leading the two Coast Guard officers down the gangway of The Emerald City. She had an arm wrapped in each of their elbows. All three of them were laughing.

Walter strode across the jetty, scattering gulls, and followed the woman back up the ramp. He realized she was older than he'd first thought, maybe thirty, maybe thirty-five; her lavender blouse seemed several sizes too small. She twisted her lips in puzzlement when he boarded the boat.

"Hey," Walter said. "Is the owner around?"

"The owner?" she asked.

"The guy with the red beard. Mr. Hold-the-Artillery."

The girl laughed. "Oh, you want Reggie. I thought you wanted Reggie's father. Total strangers come around, you know, thinking they can hit up the old man for money. They get the name off the registry at the harbormaster's, you know." The girl laughed again.

Walter didn't see what was so funny. "I want to speak to whoever it is whose cannons woke me up in the middle of the night," he said, making an effort to keep his voice steady.

"I guess you can speak to me," she said.

This offer didn't appeal to Walter; he'd been raised to think certain matters—auto-repair estimates, family loans, neighborly complaints— were the province of men. "I want to speak to Reggie."

"Reggie's kind of busy right now," she said. "But you might as well come downstairs and watch while you wait. Who knows? You might bring us good luck." The girl suddenly clasped Walter's fingers with her own and tugged him toward the stairs. Her hand was light and warm and unexpected. When they had descended into a dark corridor, she paused before a sliding door and whispered, "Please keep your voice down. Reggie's conducting a séance."

They entered a cluttered drawing room. Posters carpeted the walls, some in Cyrillic, some in German, some in an Asian language Walter didn't recognize, all vaguely left-wing and menacing. A number of busts stood around the room. On bookshelves. On end tables. None of them matched. Walter recognized Castro and Ho Chi Minh and Patrick Henry. There were also crates of musty magazines, copies of *National Geographic* from the sixties, wooden tennis rackets, a large brass cuspidor, and two brightly painted cigar-store Indians standing back-to-back. In the middle of all this, ensconced around a faded billiard table, sat the medium and his minions.

The young woman led Walter to a seat in the corner. It was actually one of four bright orange folding seats connected with iron piping. A raised metal plate read: Comiskey Park—Field Box No. 1. "It's from an old baseball stadium," she whispered. She spoke quickly, often falling short of breath; her voice reminded Walter of cloudbursts. "One of the old man's partners owned the Chicago White Sox." She twisted her lip. "Or maybe it was the Cubs."

"Silence!" the bearded man boomed. "I require complete silence."

He lifted his hands and drew with him the hands of his neighbors. They elevated their opposite hands. Eventually, the twelve participants were holding their arms outstretched with their fingers interlocking at shoulder level. All had their eyes closed. On the table before them lay a black-and-white photograph. A stern-featured bald man glared up at Walter. He sported a starched collar and Windsor tie.

"O Debs," intoned the bearded man. "O Great Debs, father

TOWARD UNCHARTED WATERS

pacifist and champion of honest labor, hear our cry!"

The girl nudged Walter. "We're celebrating Eugene Debs's birthday. You know, the socialist. It's not really his birthday, of course, but Reggie decided to condense them all. He says birthdays are arbitrary anyway. That's why we had Trotsky's last night, and we're going to do Lenin tomorrow. If we're lucky, we can get them all in before hurricane season, you know." Her voice was barely audible, and once again she punctuated her sentence with bleating laughter. Walter realized this wasn't an expression of amusement, but a nervous habit. "You probably think this is strange," she added. "That's because you're not used to it. If you try hard enough, you can get used to anything."

"I see," Walter whispered.

"O Debs," Reggie chanted. "We feel your presence, O Great One."

The girl squeezed Walter's knee; she wanted his attention. "I know who you are. You're from the television news. You're Walt the Weather Wizard! I didn't recognize you without your hot & cold cap."

Walter winced. It was the network's idea that his cap, a shade of either blue or orange, reflect the day's expected temperature.

"We used to live in D.C.," the girl said. "We watched you every morning. What a ridiculous cap, though. That must be so embarrassing."

"I got used to it," Walter said.

Reggie continued his supplications. Among his followers were the woman in the rabbit costume and her companion with the guillotine collar. There were also several older men, maybe Walter's age, their hair long and gray and wild. There was a stunning dark-skinned girl in her late teens. And—Walter wondered if Marcy would believe him—there were two men with waistcoats and monocles who each bore a striking resemblance to Theodore Roosevelt.

"I take it," Walter ventured, "that this was a costume party."

"No. That's how they normally dress."

"This is really too much," Walter said. Then he realized the girl was joking. "I guess that was a stupid thing to ask. It's not every day I end up at a Communist costume party."

"We're not Communists," said the girl. "We're Weathermen."

"You don't mean—?"

The girl shook her head. "Everybody asks that."

Walter let out his breath.

The girl crossed her legs. "It's kind of funny, how we ended up next to a real weatherman, you know. What are the odds? But Reggie says there's no such thing as coincidence. You have to think of all the times we didn't end up next to a weatherman. And how we never ended up next to the other Weathermen, the ones who really blow things up. It's like when you go to the movies and you see that the license-plate number of the getaway car matches your birthday. Pretty weird, huh? But think of all the other movies you've seen where the license plates didn't match your birthday. And think of all the other numbers in your life that this license plate didn't match—Social Security numbers and phone numbers and all. So, you know, it's really not a coincidence that we found you."

The girl laughed through her speech. Walter found her difficult to follow. All he wanted to do was to complain about the noise, to express his displeasure and leave. That was the American way. But now he was prisoner to a séance and a circular discourse on philosophy. He sneezed.

Several heads turned in his direction. Reggie opened his eyes and glared. "It doesn't work if you make noise," he snapped.

The girl clutched Walter's hand. When Reggie returned to the business of summoning the socialist—he was now swaying back and forth in a perverse mourning ritual—she said: "Don't worry about Reggie. He's just upset because they're predicting a mild hurricane season, you know. And we've come down here to experience a Category 5."

"That's a joke?" Walter asked.

"It started by accident when we were driving cross-country last summer and were picked up by a tornado. In Kansas. That's where we got the name The Emerald City. Then we did a blizzard in Newfoundland,

TOWARD UNCHARTED WATERS

but that was no big deal. And after we're done here, we're headed to California for the earthquakes. The Weathermen's creed, you know, is that the revolution will result from natural disaster." She leaned into his ear and added, "None of us really believe that, of course, except maybe Reggie, but it's lots of fun."

Reggie dropped his arms to the table; the others opened their eyes. "Jesus Christ, I give up. It's not in the atmosphere today, folks. Sorry." He turned to the girl. "For God's sake, Pam, haven't I told you not to bring strangers into the séance?"

This struck Walter as a good opening. He rose to complain, but Reggie turned away. The costumed revolutionaries paid him no attention. By the time he'd made his way to the billiard table, Reggie was already in heated conference with the two Roosevelts. "The simplest way is to use a rag and kerosene," he was saying, "but some saltpeter in a whiskey bottle can be much more effective." Walter realized the man was offering a gourmet recipe for Molotov cocktails.

Walter coughed several times, but he couldn't edge his way into the conversation. Touching Reggie, even a tap of the shoulder, didn't seem like a good idea. Soon Pam took Walter by the hand and steered him out onto the deck.

"I'm glad you stopped by," she said. "You were much more fun than the harbor patrol."

"How did you get rid of them so easily?"

"I offered them both blowjobs," she said.

Walter clutched for a railing that wasn't there. An osprey swept across the water and landed on an elevated wooden platform.

"You're something else," Pam said. "You believe everything you're told, don't you? Do we really strike you as that depraved? All I did was invite them to tomorrow's party."

"Tomorrow's party," echoed Walter.

"Stop by anytime," said Pam.

Walter nodded absently. "Maybe I will."

It wasn't until he was home, feeding Marcy her lunch of a chopped egg and a Caesar salad, that he fully appreciated the failure of his morning visit. He hadn't expressed his indignation. He hadn't even spoken to the jerk with the beard. In fact, they were going to have another party the following night. And yet in spite of this, he found he'd actually enjoyed himself aboard The Emerald City. He knew that he'd had a good time, maybe too good a time, because he kept the details of the episode from his wife.

Walter's relationship with Marcy was faltering. There was no other way to put it. Their marriage had been built upon doing things together—hiking, camping, skiing. They'd enjoyed their down time apart. This arrangement had worked wonderfully when they'd each led separate lives, when he spent ten hours a day at the network and she taught four classes a semester. Now they found that they didn't have very much to talk about. Anything at all, really. They had only memories—and those were taboo. They couldn't even escape into sex. Walter knew that it was possible for quadriplegics to have intercourse, but he didn't dare ask Marcy. Such a request struck him as selfish and vulgar, the act itself as repulsive as rape. Besides, he admitted, the black down had grown thick on Marcy's calves and across her upper lip; she'd lost weight; after a month of washing and wiping her, Walter couldn't convince himself to find her attractive.

The contrast between the two boats added to his torment. Four, five, six nights a week The Emerald City hosted late-night celebrations, festivities marked by skinny-dipping and drunken renditions of "The Internationale." The parties grew larger and louder and longer. One evening, a banner hailed the arrival of the Atlantic hurricane season. Then came painted sheets announcing the birthdays of storms Amalia, Bruno, Clarisse. Frequently, the harbor patrol visited the jetty. The owner of the Dutch windmill, a retired accountant with overgrown eyebrows, circulated a petition. Meanwhile, Walter purchased earplugs for Marcy and a small television for himself. He spent his afternoons

TOWARD UNCHARTED WATERS

as he'd once done in his youth, eyes glued to the screen, watching the swirling advance of tropical depressions. It passed the time. And in the evenings, he spied on the antics of his neighbors.

He grew to like Pam: the lilt of her neck when she laughed, the carefree affection she showered on strangers, the sashay of her behind in tight cutoff jeans. Their boats were moored only yards apart, and Walter sat for hours at the porthole in the galley watching her play hostess. He longed to crash one of these parties. Heck, it wouldn't even be crashing. Hadn't she told him to drop by anytime? A few of the guests who visited The Emerald City each evening with red carnations in their lapels were his age, maybe even older, and they seemed to blend. But these men didn't have Marcy to look after. Walter recalled his wife's terror when she thought he might kill her, and he couldn't bear the idea of her waking up all alone. So he envied the revelers their easy money and easy good looks and free-gushing cheer, especially because, even before his wife's injuries, he and Marcy had always been a couple for whom life and love did not flow easily. Maybe because Walter didn't want to expose his wife to the romping of his neighbors—or maybe because he didn't want the girl to see his wife—he found himself regularly concealing Marcy on the far side of the boat.

And then the girl sought him out. They were celebrating the onslaught of Diego, sawing its way across the ocean, raising warnings from Cedar Key to Port Charlotte. The storm had already hopped up the Windward Islands, clobbered Hispaniola. A mudslide in Santo Domingo had swept a children's hospital over a precipice. Walter tried to form a connection between the wailing, blood-soaked mothers on the television screen and the confetti-tossing partygoers on the neighboring boat. He watched as one of the former Theodore Roosevelts tottered on the roof of the motorized vessel holding a wine glass aloft and shouting, "Batten down the hatches! I say, boys, lash me to the mizzen mast!"

Walter jolted at the rap on the cabin door. He pulled his head from the porthole.

Pam appeared at the break in the bulkhead, holding a pink ladies' shoe with a broken heel in one hand. "You ready to come out and play?"

"I was just seeing what the noise was."

"You were just spying on us again, Walt the Weather Wizard. Like you do every night. But now Reggie wants you. He wants to ask you some questions."

"That's not really a good idea," he said. "I have to keep an eye on my wife. She's not well." But while he protested, Walter picked up his gray parka and fishing hat, and when Pam insisted, he followed her sumptuous derrière onto the neighboring vessel.

They found Reggie standing on the binnacle. A small crowd had followed him into the wheelhouse, where he was speaking at them with vehemence. "Sure, God gives Job more sons and daughters, but they're different sons and daughters. Doesn't that strike you as troubling? And a different wife, too. So the poor righteous fool ends up with a new wife and new kids and he's supposed to be happy?"

One man muttered: "I'll take some new kids."

"And a new wife!"

There was laughter all around.

Reggie called for silence by slapping an iron wrench against the helm. "So the bottom line is that if they don't remove their Bible-thumping opium-of-the-masses take-my-name-in-vein billboard, Ma Nature's going to do it for them. Right, Diego?"

Someone flicked the lights on and off. The crowd cheered.

"Let's ask our resident expert," Reggie suggested. "Walt, what do you think?"

All eyes focused on Walter.

"About what?"

"About Diego, my man. Do you think he has it in him?"

Walter paused at the ambiguity of the question. "It's a very dangerous storm," he ventured. "I suspect it may do some heavy damage."

"Get that man a drink," Reggie ordered. "Make it a double."

TOWARD UNCHARTED WATERS

A rangy young guy with a permanently hangdog look proposed a series of toasts to Walter's health and welfare. Several seconds later, the former rabbit-woman lassoed him with a lei. Somehow he found himself wearing a conical hat with the stunning dark-skinned girl sitting on his lap and the crowd saluting him in the discordant strains of "For He's a Jolly Good Fellow."

After that, the crowd's attention shifted to a man chasing a St. Bernard across the deck with a trombone. Walter searched the vessel for Pam, hoping to thank her for the invitation. The mob in the cabin proved too thick to penetrate, and he left, dejected. It didn't make him feel any better that at midnight, and again at three o'clock, he had to wake up to shift Marcy onto her opposite side.

Diego fizzled out in the Gulf of Mexico. Walter returned for more parties. He stole away after Marcy fell asleep each night, for a few minutes, for a few hours. Occasionally, when some heavy passages from the diaries of John Hanning Speke put Marcy to sleep, he also sneaked off during the afternoon. The Babcocks—it turned out they were married—appeared happy for his company. Pam quizzed him on his experiences in broadcasting, and Reggie sought out his meteorological expertise. It surprised and pleased Walter to discover that while they had many acquaintances—vacationers willing to fire their cannon, local radicals up for mooching their booze— they didn't have friends.

Reggie explained their circumstances over Rob Roys. "I know an awful lot, my man," he said. "That scares most people off."

"He has only two moods," Pam said. "Drunk and knowledgeable, and sober and irritable. It's the drunk and knowledgeable I married him for. I have a thing for intensely smart men."

Reggie did seem to possess a great deal of information. He spoke easily on the geology of South Florida and the physics of billiards and the epidemiology of tropical ailments. Walter understood how this fellow might leave a man feeling inadequate.

"It's too bad you never bring your wife over," Pam said.

Walter gulped down his drink. "She's not well."

Pam twisted her lip. "Oh, you mean she's really not well."

"She doesn't go out among people."

Walter still took pains to conceal Marcy from his neighbors. Somehow her injuries were like a badge of shame that he feared might lead to his own banishment.

Pam nodded sympathetically. "I guess it's hard when you're in a wheelchair."

"How did you know that?"

"We know everything." Pam laughed. "And what we don't know, we make up."

A patch of dark stratus clouds covered the sun. Walter shivered.

"You should bring her over sometime," Pam said. "I promise we'll be on our best behavior. Won't we, darling?"

"Scout's honor," promised Reggie. He kissed his wife's hand.

These moments of intimacy were a blot on Walter's happiness. They reminded him that Reggie and Pam slept together in the same bed. Otherwise, it would have been possible to love both of them. But he wanted Pam. He didn't even think of her and his own wife in competition. Loving Pam would mean sleeping with a body, while loving Marcy meant caring for a head.

Reggie strode to the wet bar and mixed himself another drink. "I read somewhere that when Einstein taught at Yale, the university hired a graduate student to follow him around and write down everything he said on the off-chance he might say something brilliant. Sometimes I think they should do the same for Reginald Babcock." There wasn't even a hint of humor in Reggie's voice. He polished off his glass with one swig. "So tell me, Walt, what do you think of Graciella?"

"It's still hard to tell," Walter said. "I'm not evacuating just yet."

"Evacuating? Don't be nuts, my man. I have good feelings about Old Gracie. We're counting on you to be the guest of honor at our landfall party."

"If they put up the order," Walter said, "I'm bailing out."

"What are you so afraid of?" Pam asked. "Hurricanes are predictable. Reggie says that if you take the right precautions, you'll be okay."

"Sometimes the right precaution is to leave."

Pam squeezed Walter's knee under the table. "We were talking last night and decided hurricanes just aren't our match. What we really need is something with guns. You don't know anywhere we could find a bank robbery, do you? Or a good old-fashioned holdup?"

"No," Walter said stiffly. "I don't."

"Too bad. We had such high hopes for you."

Walter rose to go. "Marcy and I were once in a hurricane," he said. "Eloise. Back in '75. We were honeymooning in the Yucatan. Never in my entire life have I seen such destruction. Whole towns carried out into the Gulf. Trust me. When they issue the warning, pack up and go."

Reggie followed Walter to the gangway and rested a large palm on his shoulder. "Now it's my turn to offer advice," he said.

Walter waited uncomfortably. The Eleanor Roosevelt's flag flapped against a gray sky.

Reggie pointed across the jetty.

"That's a cockamamie way to moor a houseboat for a hurricane," he said. "You're tied up tight like you're crowding into an anchorage at Nantucket or the Vineyard. You need to loosen her up a bit down here, give her a few yards of slack. Otherwise, your lines will snap."

"I had no idea," Walter said.

"Of course you didn't."

Reggie retied Walter's boat.

"Old Gracie, baby," he said. "I can feel it in my goddamn bones."

⁊

A NERVOUS HUSH DESCENDED upon Pelican Bay. It infected the proprietors boarding up windows on Nautilus Boulevard and the state troopers sandbagging at the waterfront and even the roseate spoonbills and wood storks roosting in the pine barrens overlooking the bay. The exodus of tourists from the barrier islands brought Interstate traffic to a standstill. Two harbor-patrol squad vans crisscrossed the downtown blaring commands through mounted bullhorns:

AN EVACUATION ORDER HAS BEEN ISSUED FOR CORMORANT COUNTY. PLEASE BE ADVISED. AN EVACUATION ORDER HAS BEEN ISSUED FOR CORMORANT COUNTY. PLEASE BE ADVISED.

By nightfall, the houseboat shaped like a Dutch windmill had departed.

Walter stayed. There was no urgency. He rigged an extension cord to the TV set and sat on the deck watching Graciella churn its way across the screen. Sometimes he flipped off the coverage and stared up at the billboard. For some reason, he thought more and more about the women's soccer team; he pictured the girls on the airplane, in matching uniforms, jetting over the great blue ocean. They had their whole lives ahead of them. Uncharted waters. And only six weeks before, a mere heartbeat, he and Marcy had joked about the team's highway sign.

The first raindrops fell two days later. It was Marcy's fiftieth birthday. She'd just gone through the perilously awkward routine of making wishes and blowing out candles on a cake.

Walter let the sea air fill his lungs; he looked at his watch. The previous afternoon, despite the protestations of Reggie Babcock, he'd packed up the car.

"I think now's the time," he said to Marcy. "Are you ready?"

Marcy's face looked blotchy and shrunken like a crabapple. "I'm up for anything," she said, "as long as we're together."

"I'm bringing along Speke's book on Tanganyika," Walter said. "If I'm not too tired when we get to a shelter, I'll read to you some."

"That would be nice," said Marcy. "As long as we stay together."

Walter wondered if she intended anything extra by these words.

"Of course we'll be together," he said. "I'm just going to say goodbye to that couple on the next boat, and then we're off." This was the first time he'd ever alluded directly to the Babcocks, but he was just being neighborly. You couldn't fault a man for being neighborly, now could you?

Marcy said nothing. Walter walked briskly to The Emerald City without looking back.

He drew aside a mauve curtain inscribed WELCOME HOME GABBY and stepped into the dim recesses of the Babcocks' boat. He hadn't been on board unchaperoned before. Taking this liberty somehow augmented the intimacy of their triangle.

"Reggie!" he shouted. "Reggie? Pam?"

He slid open the door to the drawing room.

Pam Babcock was standing on tiptoes atop the billiard table. Coils of pink and red streamers were wrapped around one of her arms, and she held a stapler above her head in the other. She wore only a skin-colored towel; fine rivulets of water trickled from her wet hair and down her back. Walter took in the silky smoothness of her legs and underarms.

Walter rapped his knuckles on a cabinet.

"Just the man I was looking for," Pam said. She walked to the edge of the table and extended her sleek, bare arms for Walter to help her down. Her bare feet landed with a baby-hop. "We're pushing up our fiesta by a day. It's looking like landfall before dawn."

"That's why I stopped by," Walter said. "We're going. Is Reggie around?"

Pam shook her head. "He went to town to buy more beer." She twisted her lips. "You can't go, Walt the Weather Wizard. You're our guest of honor. I've been counting on you."

"It's not safe. You should get out, too."

"We made it through a tornado."

"Hurricanes aren't tornadoes."

Pam laughed. Walter felt good. "Can you at least help me with the decorations?" she asked. "Reggie was supposed to help me, but we had a fight."

Walter climbed onto the table and began fastening ribbon to the ceiling. He listened while Pam recounted every detail of the Babcocks' morning spat—the sarcastic quips, the shattered china—but when she'd finished, Walter wasn't exactly sure what the couple had fought about.

"Sometimes Reggie can be so immature," Pam said. "Sometimes I wish I'd married an older man." She handed Walter the last of the streamer rolls, and her fingers brushed his wrist; he felt his erection grow.

"All done," said Walter, slapping his hands together. "That was easy enough."

"Now all I have to do is convince you to stay for our party tonight." The water trickled down Pam's neck, into her cleavage. "I always get what I want, you know. That's something you should know about me."

Walter struggled down from the table. "But what if you don't?"

She shrugged her delicate shoulders. "But I do."

She inched forward and blew the words into Walter's face: "I always do."

Walter beamed.

He retreated to the Eleanor Roosevelt and told Marcy that he thought they should brave out the storm. Marcy responded with a tight-lipped frown. Then she asked him if he wouldn't please straighten her kerchief.

೦೨

BY THE TIME THE FIRST GUESTS ARRIVED, the wind had picked up and the rain seemed to be blowing in horizontal pellets. Walter held fast to a drainage pipe on the leeward side of the vessel and watched as Reggie unfurled a banner welcoming the tempest. They exchanged greetings; the words were lost to the surf. The former rabbit-woman and former Marie Antoinette arrived—Walter now knew they were a couple—and they were followed by both former Roosevelts and the trombone player with the spirited St. Bernard. The guests quickly vanished below deck. Walter checked the wind speed and the barometric pressure every few minutes. He could no longer see the billboard. Soon he could barely discern the outline of the Babcocks' boat.

He fed Marcy another piece of birthday cake. He attempted to read her to sleep, but the toss and turn of the boat made sleep impossible. "I'm going to go up top," he finally said. "Just for a few minutes."

"Please don't," Marcy said. "Not tonight."

"I promise I'll be right back."

Outside, several bodies of royal terns lay lifeless on the deck. Walter slid one into the water with his foot, and the bloody feathers clumped on his shoe. The vessel rose and fell like an angry beast trying to shake Walter from its back. He let the wind carry him along the jetty and up the gangway of The Emerald City, where Pam assisted him through the hatch. Her bangs dangled from under a rhinestone tiara, and she carried a glass of champagne.

"It's about time," she said.

Walter squeezed the water from his eyes. "That's one mean wind."

"Don't get all technical on me," Pam said.

Walter stepped past her toward the partially open door of the drawing room, but she tugged his hand in the opposite direction.

"If I have to hear Reggie talk about the Southampton Hurricane one more time," she said, "I don't know what I'll do. You know, I mean what I'll really do." The cabin lurched backward on a heavy wave. Pam caught her balance against Walter's chest. For the first time, he realized that she was drunk. "I know where we can go," she said.

They entered a cozy chamber; it might have passed for a stateroom on a cruise ship. There were mahogany bureaus, three spider plants hanging at the portholes, a watercolor study of pheasants. No Soviet propaganda, no portraits of Mao. Pam threw her body across the bed, slapped the bedspread, and invited Walter to join her.

"This is the old man's room," she explained. "It's the condition for letting us use the boat. He hasn't actually visited, you know, but he is always threatening." She dug both pillows out from under the covers and used them to bolster her back.

Walter edged his way onto the bed. The chandeliers swayed. Through the cabin walls, he heard Reggie taunting the storm.

Pam flipped onto her stomach and kicked up her legs. "So tell me about you," she said. "I mean really tell me about you."

"What do you want me to tell you?"

"Everything interesting," she said. "That's what I do, you know. I milk all the knowledge out of people."

"And when you're done?"

Pam giggled. "I get rid of them." She propped herself up on her bare elbows. "I know. Why don't you tell me about your wife?"

"I don't think that's such a good idea," Walter said.

"Please," said Pam. "I told you I always get what I want. You wouldn't want to ruin my track record, now would you? Pretty please."

"She was a zoologist," said Walter reluctantly. "She's studied African ungulates. Okapis. Sometimes they're also known as forest jackasses, but they're not." He explained how early expeditions under Sclater and Johnson had mistakenly thought the animal a donkey, how they'd dismissed the Mbutis' tales of foot-long tongues and cloven hooves as so much rubbish. He explained the peculiar digestive habits of ruminants. He told her of the parasitic worms that were driving the species to extinction. It amazed him how fluidly he could speak on a subject about which he thought he knew so little. Pam lay on her back and stared up at him while he talked.

"But the most amazing thing about the okapi are their breeding habits," Walter said. He stopped uncomfortably, not wanting to continue. Through the wall, he heard Reggie relating the history of the Southampton Hurricane. The image of Marcy flashed through Walter's thoughts: young, vibrant Marcy posing before a herd of blesbok. He shook his head violently to concentrate.

"Yes?" prodded Pam.

"They lick each other. They lick each other's entire bodies from head to toe. From horns to hooves. From, well, all over."

"That must be fun," Pam laughed. "But messy."

She started to sit up, but the boat reeled suddenly. A bookcase pitched forward in the corner. Walter found himself with one of his arms around the girl's back and the other curled awkwardly against her chest. He pressed his lips into hers. Reggie ranted behind the paneling. She kissed back.

Without warning, she pushed him away. "I'm sorry. I don't want this."

Walter heard the sharp edge to her voice. He relaxed his grip on her back.

"You're almost twice my age," Pam said. She drew herself out of his grasp and brushed the creases from her dress. She laughed. Walter sensed his anger mounting. "Let's go check on Reggie and the others," she suggested.

Walter didn't move. He let his body rise and fall with the bed. Through the paneling, he listened to Reggie charming his guests with the legends of Diane, Audrey, Camille. "This is nothing," said Reggie. "Imagine what it was like in the days before forecasting, in the days of uncharted waters. Take the Hurricane of 1922, for example. She submerged all of Cormorant Island. The entire city of Pelican Bay washed into the Gulf." The boat jolted forward and ceiling lights flickered.

Look, I'm sorry," Pam said. "C'mon. You're not going to ruin the party just because I'm not willing to kiss you. Let's go next door and have some fun."

Walter stood up. "It's bullshit. Total bullshit."

"You're not being fair," Pam said.

Walter walked past her and stepped into the smoky drawing room. He braced himself against the billiard table for balance. Across the room,

Reggie sat on the bar wearing a plastic Viking helmet and fondling a mixed drink.

"Our expert," Reggie greeted him. "And my darling wife."

"It's bullshit," Walter repeated, louder. "There was no Hurricane of 1922. Not around here."

"What's that?" Reggie asked.

"You just say whatever comes into your head," Walter said. "Whatever suits your purpose at a given moment." He turned toward Pam. "Both of you."

"My man, my man," Reggie said. "I'm sure this is some sort of misunderstanding."

Reggie tried to wrap his arm around Walter's shoulder; Walter shook him off.

"It's no misunderstanding. You're a goddamned fraud." Walter sensed that he was speaking much too loud. The partygoers were staring at him uncomfortably. They clearly thought he was drunk.

"Gayle, my man," Reggie said. "If you're lucky, you won't remember this in the morning. Now why don't I walk you home. You didn't bring a jacket, did you?"

"I'll go home when I'm ready to go home. I don't need your help."

He rode the undulations of the boat toward the door; a powerful breaker tossed him headlong down the corridor and through the hatch. When he regained his balance, Reggie and Pam had followed him out onto the deck.

"What the fuck's gotten into you, Gayle?" Reggie demanded.

"Please, Walt," Pam begged. "Don't, Reggie."

"Leave me alone," Walter shouted. He rounded the corner of the deckhouse; a wind gust picked him up and threw him back against the iron siding. Spray blew in every direction. He held one hand over his eyes and squinted through the stabs of rain. His entire body started to tremble.

Suddenly, the wind died, and across the inlet a panel of moonlight cut a shaft through the black. All around him hung the despotic silence of the eye.

"What the fuck, Gayle?" Reggie demanded, then paused: "Wait. Where's your boat?"

The Eleanor Roosevelt's berth lay empty; the mooring lines squirmed on the surface like eels. Off in the distance, three hundred yards out, four hundred yards, a dark form drifted toward the open waters. It might have been the silhouette of the Gayles' vessel; it might have been almost anything. In the murk, it was impossible to tell.

"Oh, my man," said Reggie. "I'm sorry. I'm so sorry."

He slapped Walter's shoulder with his open palm.

Walter clambered over the railing. He plunged into the opaque water and swam violently, stroke after stroke, toward the drifting shadow, out of the eye of the storm. •

Rendezvous in Wikiternity

DANA WHITLOCK WAS NOT EVEN remotely famous, and despite the prophecy of the winged monkey with the Ouija board, the thirty-six-year-old actress was grounded enough to recognize that stardom no longer awaited her. So when the Scarecrow appeared in her dressing room with his laptop set to her Wikipedia entry, she instantly suspected her new acquaintance of chicanery. Ian Docherty, a rough-hewn, fifty-something Scottish expat, partial to cashmere scarves and spicy gossip, struck her as charming, but slippery, and she didn't put it past him to enshrine her in cyberspace for his own amusement. "You're going to transform me from a good witch into a bad witch very quickly if you don't shut that thing off," she threatened, adjusting her auburn wig in a mirror bisected by a jagged horizontal scar. "Can't you find some birds to frighten?"

"Not in this hellhole, darling," replied Docherty, settling his straw-packed rump into a battle-splintered captain's chair and lighting a cigarette. "Any creature with a brain the size of a walnut was smart enough to fly this coop ages ago."

"Watch it, mister. You're talking about my hometown," warned Dana, unable to suppress a grin. "And would you put that goddamn cigarette out? You can light your ass on fire, for all I care. Just do it far away from my voicebox."

Docherty answered with a perfectly formed ring of blue-tinged smoke. "I'll make you a deal, darling," he offered. "You tell me all about Caleb, and then your friendly neighborhood fag-with-a-fag will let your precious vocal chords live to sing another day."

"Who's Caleb?"

"Playing dumb, are we? It says right here that '*Miss Whitlock has been romantically linked to attorney Caleb Belding.*' So spill it, baby. Who's Caleb?"

"Let me see that," Dana demanded. She crouched down from the knees, careful not to dislodge her rhinestone crown, and read over Docherty's shoulder:

> Dana Whitlock (b. February 21, 1973, in Creve Coeur, Rhode Island) is an American character actress known for her great beauty and versatility. She graduated from Roger Williams High School in Creve Coeur and attended the New York Stage and Film Academy. Whitlock is currently starring as Glinda, the Good Witch of the North, in a regional production of *The Wizard of Oz*. She lives in New York City.
>
> Miss Whitlock has been romantically linked to attorney Caleb Belding.

Dana eyed the strawman suspiciously. She'd only known Docherty for three weeks, and she couldn't imagine how he'd have discovered her birth date—her *real* birth date, not the more recent one that she affixed to the back of her headshots.

"So?" Docherty wore a roguish smirk. "Who's Caleb?"

Dana plucked the cigarette from his fingers and crushed it beneath her satin slipper.

"Who's Caleb?" she snapped. "I have no fucking idea."

NEITHER DANA NOR DOCHERTY had any clue how to edit a Wikipedia entry—a process not intuitive to a pair of self-proclaimed Luddites who didn't even own cell phones—so Professor Marvel was already dispatching Dorothy back to Auntie Em when Dana finally figured out how to expunge her alleged liaison with Caleb Belding from the website. She considered replacing the line with another that read:

> Miss Whitlock is in a serious relationship with actor Jayson Rex Steinberg.

But she wasn't too sure that her year-long romance with Jayson was, in fact, serious. Not in a *permanent* way, or even that it would survive her eight-week gig in Creve Coeur, so instead she merely pared out the offending language, advanced her date of birth three years, and hurried onto the stage—*sans* magic wand—to greet the former Miss Teen Massachusetts, a would-be starlet who displayed a shameless knack for overplaying the show's leading role. Not that anybody in the audience of grade-school students and chaperones ever noted such nuance. The previous afternoon, when Dana had asked the *Oz*-struck Dorothy whether she was a "good witch" or a "bad witch," an overweight kid in the front row had bellowed out, "She's a sandwich!" That proved the only laugh-line of the performance. But the Good Witch gave herself over to her labors—even if a children's musical in a moribund industrial hub wasn't exactly the stuff from which dreams are spun—and after Miss Mass. clicked her heels together three times, with the force of clashing cymbals, Dana retreated to her dressing room primed for a hot bath and a cup of tea. Instead, she discovered Ian Docherty, laptop in hand, perched on her make-up counter.

"I'm afraid Miss Whitlock is *again* romantically linked to attorney Caleb Belding," he announced. And it was true—according to the computer, at least. "You also received a message on your account asking you not to erase content without providing an explanation."

This was too much for Dana. Returning to Creve Coeur for the first time in eighteen years had forced her to take stock of herself—and while she wasn't certain about what she'd dreamed of in high school, when she'd starred in her senior-class production of *Our Town*—she knew it wasn't to return to half-empty matinees and seventh billing in a theater slated to be razed for a shopping mall at the end of the run. She took the part because she needed the work, pure and simple, but hadn't anticipated the stage-door greetings from the children of former classmates—classmates who asked after the health of her deceased parents and invited her to restaurants a stratosphere beyond her budget. All she had to show for herself were crow's feet, and an unstable relationship, and now a throbbing headache above her left temple.

"I'll give them an explanation!" Dana cried. "Show me where I type it."

Docherty whistled at her anger, but called up the appropriate screen. He watched in bemused awe as Dana, who'd once taken a secretarial skills course, vented her wrath at seventy-five words per minute.

> Miss Whitlock is NOT romantically linked to Caleb Belding, because Miss Whitlock has never heard of Mr. Belding. NEVER EVER EVER! Furthermore, Miss Whitlock doesn't care if this is an honest mistake, or a hoax, or some sick loser's deranged fantasy, but it has to stop right now. Immediately! Am I making myself clear????

Dana reloaded the "talk page" multiple times, to make certain that her message had been posted, then ordered Docherty to remove the inaccurate text from the article itself. Meanwhile, she stepped behind the folding screen and slid out of her vintage pink gown, grateful to be free from the heavy gingham sleeves. And how dare anyone call her a "character" actress? Hadn't she wowed the Berkshires as Hedda Gabler only three summers earlier?

"Would you like me to revise your age again, too?" Docherty called.

"Go throw yourself into a burning barn," she hollered back. "And yes! Please do!"

Soon she was strolling along Hutchinson Boulevard in her street clothes, linked at the elbows with Docherty and Vince Pepper, the Ouija-wielding winged monkey who'd predicted her impending fame at the cast party, the three of them heading toward the renovated waterfront flophouse that the production company rented as an Equity dorm. She'd already settled into a foam bath—in the living space that she shared with Miss Mass.—when the phone rang.

"It's *person-to-person* for you," said Miss. Mass, whose real name was Tiffany, handing Dana the portable console. "Who ever heard of calling *person-to-person*?"

Dana held her wet palm over the receiver. "Who is it?" she whispered.

"Person-to-person," repeated Tiffany—as though this were a social *faux pas*, like wearing suspenders, that rendered the caller perpetually un-cool. "For Miss Dana Whitlock from Mr. Caleb Belding."

Caleb Belding! An electric appliance falling into the tub could not have jolted Dana's spine as viciously as the attorney's name. She drew a deep breath and removed her hand from the receiver.

"Hello? Caleb?" she asked, not allowing the caller an opportunity to respond. "I don't know who you are or what you want, but whatever your game is, I'm not interested. Now if you don't leave me alone, I'm going to phone the police."

"Heavens, darling, you need to chill out," replied an unfazed Ian Docherty. "I just called to wish you a good night."

"You're an asshole."

"That's not a wholly original suggestion."

She could hear Docherty munching on junk food while he spoke.

"And you posted that article about me online, too, didn't you?"

"I swear I did not. Upon the graves of all my straw ancestors."

Something about Docherty kept her from telling him off in earnest. Maybe it was that she sensed a deep sadness pooled inside the middle-aged dancer—a well of suffering beneath his charm and antics—and any attempt to pierce it would have been as cruel as prying the shell off a tortoise. With regard to the Internet posting, her instinct told her to believe his denials.

Once she'd lathered her face with nourishing lotion, she phoned her boyfriend in New York and told him all about the Wikipedia episode.

"Who's Ian?" Jayson asked, curiosity cloaked in nonchalance.

He didn't ask: *Who's Caleb Belding?* Not: *Did she feel safe?* But he also didn't object when she left town for eight weeks at a stretch, or performed summer stock in the sticks, not easy qualities to find in a lover who still possesses all his own teeth.

She had described the Scotsman to Jayson several times already, explained that Docherty lived only blocks away from her in Brooklyn—alone, since his partner had died. "Ian is my *gay* friend who plays the Scarecrow," she said. "Why don't you ever listen to a word I say?"

"Because I'm an actor, baby," Jayson said. "I'm used to doing the talking. I leave the listening to the people who pay for tickets."

⁓

BREAKFAST THE NEXT DAY, at the Waffle Pantry across from the theater, found Docherty ranting against the show's producers, a Boston-based team named Lowery & Bratton that kept themselves at arm's length from the performers. "That damn bed is practically made of barbed wire," he complained—for the twentieth straight morning. "You could fillet Bratton like a snapper, and I swear to you, you wouldn't find a fragment of honest bone in the man's corpse."

Vince, the winged monkey, rolled his eyes. The square-faced wardrobe mistress who completed their foursome pinched a French fry from the Scarecrow's plate.

"My boyfriend is jealous of you," Dana said.

"It's your lawyer friend that he should be jealous of," replied Docherty, wrenching a bite from a rubbery bagel. "As of about an hour ago, you're linked to Squire Belding once more. And you've received an official warning from another editor to watch your tone."

If this revelation caught Dana off guard, it did not appear to surprise either Vince or the wardrobe mistress, both of whom had clearly been well briefed in advance by Docherty.

"How exactly does this work?" inquired the winged monkey. "Can I link myself romantically to Judy Garland and Joan Crawford?"

"This isn't funny," Dana objected, although suddenly it *did* seem funny, a bizarre and unnerving menace bordering on hilarity. "I swear if any of you make a joke out of this, I'm going to scream right here in the restaurant."

Docherty patted the back of her hand. "I'm sorry," he said. "I didn't realize this was genuinely upsetting you."

"What if Belding scares off my future husband?" Dana asked. "What if Mr. Right looks me up on Wikipedia and decides to ask out someone else?"

"Excuse me," interjected the winged monkey. "I thought you already had a boyfriend."

"That's not the point. *He* doesn't know that?"

"He?"

"Caleb Belding." She examined herself in her pocket mirror to make sure that none of her omelet remained preserved on her face. "You do think he's a real person, don't you?"

"How should I know?" asked Docherty, depositing a twenty-dollar bill onto the tabletop. "I don't even have a brain."

"I've got it!" Dana clapped hers hands together with enthusiasm, rattling the cutlery and nearly toppling her water glass with her elbow. "We could look him up in the phonebook."

"Or you could enter the twenty-first century, my dear, and search for him online," Vince suggested.

"And *then* what?" Docherty asked.

"I don't know. I could call the police."

"And tell them that a stranger—or someone else, because you don't even know it's him—has been editing your Wikipedia entry. *Puh-lease.*" The Scarecrow swatted the air dramatically with his hand. "You'll end up like one of those whackjobs who calls 9-1-1 when she's served the wrong dessert at McDonald's."

But Dana insisted. They had an eleven o'clock performance that morning—a private show to edify St. Trofimena's Academy for Girls—which gave Docherty just enough time to search for Belding online while Miss Mass. cavorted across the stage with her aunt and uncle.

"I do hope you appreciate this, darling," the Scarecrow said. "It's not every guy who's willing to help a woman stalk her stalker."

Dana paced the actors' lounge nervously. "Did you find him yet?"

"Bingo!" Docherty announced. "Caleb G. Belding. Associate Professor of Law at Rhode Island State University in Creve Coeur. He's cute, too."

The man certainly wasn't *un*handsome—a fair-skinned, strong-jawed all-American boy who wrote articles with two-sentence titles that Dana didn't quite understand. The gist of his expertise appeared to be in copyright and trademark litigation. BA from Brown, JD from Yale. He had even included a photograph of his twin nieces on his official university homepage. Not exactly what she'd anticipated in her stalker and, quite frankly, not the worst guy in the world to be linked with romantically. Assuming, of course, some depraved third party wasn't behind this persistent nuisance. Yet in her gut, Dana remained confident that Caleb Belding—for whatever perverse reason—had posted the article himself.

"Happy?" asked Docherty.

"Not yet. We have to go see him."

"No way." Docherty shut down the computer. "*That's* crazy."

"The second that curtain falls, you're driving me over to Rhode Island State," she said. "Caleb is about to discover that he's been harassing the wrong gal."

"I wouldn't exactly call it *harassing*."

Dana shook her fist at him. "One more word, mister, and you're going to find yourself on the wrong end of a cigarette lighter."

"Okay, but it's your funeral."

"Yes, it is. So keep your mouth shut and drive the hearse."

✧

THE "HEARSE" WAS MORE ACCURATELY a twenty-five-year-old Pontiac Bonneville that Docherty had borrowed from his late sister's husband for his stint in Creve Coeur. Warning lights blinked furiously on the dashboard every time they hit a pothole, and the transmission rumbled like a colonial lumber mill, but the vehicle hadn't cost Docherty a dime—and it conveyed the Scotsman where he wanted to go. Or, in this case, where Dana demanded that he chauffeur her. She hadn't even afforded him an opportunity to change out of his straw-packed costume, because she didn't want to lose her nerve, so they drove to the law school looking like a pair of refugees from a masquerade ball.

"Why should I care what I'm wearing?" Dana demanded. "If *he* thinks *I'm* a nutcase, so much the better!"

"This is *such* a bad idea," Docherty pleaded. "If you really want the man to go away, the best tactic is to ignore him."

But Docherty protested a bit too much, and Dana suspected that he was enjoying himself.

"I swear I'm going to thatch a roof with you," she said.

The Scarecrow sighed. "I'm just saying...."

They arrived at the university five minutes later. The campus had been laid out by a functionalist architect named Barthelme in the 1960s, so the law school's administrative headquarters resembled a lopsided rabbit hutch. Belding's office occupied part of a fifth-floor suite in Roger Williams Hall, where a walleyed secretary impeded their path. The woman had her hair curled into a pageboy flip, like a Kennedy-era model, and she exuded a vibe of marinated displeasure.

"Professor Belding sees students by appointment only," she explained—remarkably indifferent to their costumes—and flicked open a leather-bound appointment book. "You are students, aren't you? I can set you up for something late next week."

"We're *not* students," Dana said, "We'd like to see Professor Belding this afternoon. Tell him it's Miss Dana Whitlock."

"Does he know you?"

"Let's just say I've been romantically linked with him in the past."

The secretary practically peeled the flesh off Dana's face with her glare, and then asked them to wait in the reception alcove. She disappeared around the panels of her cubicle, leaving them alone with a mousy law student waiting for another faculty member. The young woman clearly wondered what they intended, dressed as they were, but she didn't dare ask.

"Talk about bureaucracy," Docherty whispered. "What kind of world do we live in where you have to take a number to meet your own stalker?"

A moment later, the secretary—sour as ever—ushered them into Belding's office. The law professor was as clean-cut in person as he appeared on the Internet, although his hair had grayed prematurely since he'd been photographed. He wore a tweed jacket with elbow patches, and thin-rimmed spectacles. *Certainly not unhandsome.* But he greeted Dana and Docherty with a slight lisp, and his manner was ungainly.

"My goodness. Dana Whitlock in my office," he said, rising behind his cluttered desk. "I didn't really expect you to show up here."

Dana gave him no time to adjust. "So you *did* write that about me online."

"Goodness," Belding stammered. "I wondered if I'd hear from you at some point…."

"Well, you're hearing from me *now*," snapped Dana, brandishing her silver wand. "You can't just go around slandering innocent strangers and expect them to take it sitting down."

The law professor looked deflated. "You don't know who I am, do you?"

"Should I?"

Belding shook his head. "Well, I suppose this is my own damn fault," he said, and he raised his eyebrows inquisitively at Docherty.

"Don't mind me," the Scotsman said. "I'm her duenna."

The lawyer nodded, unsurprised, as though all actresses traveled under supervision.

"Give me one moment," he apologized. "I was just preparing for a teleconference." Then he summoned the walleyed secretary via the intercom and instructed her to delay his long-distance meeting for half an hour. By the time he returned his focus to Dana, who, in the interim, had an opportunity to eyeball his diplomas and safari photographs and countless letters of appreciation from the ACLU and the National Organization for Women, some of her anger had dissipated.

"Look, I didn't mean to cause you any anxiety," Belding said. "It's just that I took my nieces to *The Wizard of Oz* last week, and somehow, the coincidence of seeing you again like that, I don't know…. Maybe I thought that creating a Wikipedia entry for you would generate some sort of connection between us…. It was foolish."

"Seeing me *again*?"

"You really don't remember, do you? I played Joe Stoddard in *Our Town*. The undertaker. In *high school*. I asked you out after the last show, and you blew me off."

That was all perfectly plausible. She'd blown off lots of guys at eighteen—even the hockey captain who portrayed George Gibbs—blissfully unaware of the pain she was inflicting. But why should she bear the blame if every acne-pocked schoolboy in Rhode Island had seemed to want a piece of her? The bottom line was that she had absolutely no memory of this middle-aged man whom she'd rejected as a teenager, presumably out of carelessness, not malevolence. She certainly didn't owe him anything, not after half a lifetime.

"So now that you're here," said Belding, flashing a magnetic smile, "what do you say? Can I buy you dinner?"

Dana thought she'd misheard him. "You cannot be serious."

"Why not? You came all the way out here to meet me, didn't you? You must have been the least bit curious."

Not curious, thought Dana. *Frustrated. Beset.* But how was she supposed to convince a man who taught other people how to argue for a living?

"Besides," the litigator added, "I've always had a soft spot for beautiful witches."

Dana felt herself blushing. "Maybe if you'd asked me out in person like a normal human being instead of making up nonsense about me on the Internet…."

"If I had asked you out, would you have said yes?"

His open face was full of hope. In the corridor, a vacuum cleaner whirred.

"I don't know," she answered, suddenly feeling flustered and inarticulate. "I mean: No. No, I wouldn't have. Because I have a boyfriend…. And that's not the point anyway, since you *didn't* ask me out like a normal human being."

"Isn't that what I'm doing now? Or *trying* to, at least."

Belding's voice had acquired an unmistakably heartfelt sincerity, and he leaned toward her over the mahogany desk with his splayed fingers braced against the blotter. There was no denying that some lucky woman would indeed be very fortunate to snag Caleb G. Belding, Associate Professor of Law, even if his mating rituals proved unorthodox. But Belding also struck her as the kind of man who wanted his partner in one place—with him—and that place was, regrettably, the culturally comatose city of Creve Coeur.

Dana shook her head. "It's too late. I'm sorry."

"Think it over, okay?"

"There's nothing to think over. It was a pleasure to have met you, Caleb, but now I'm going to have to ask you to stop slandering me online."

She motioned for Docherty to exit and followed him through the open door, nearly tearing her gauze hem on the exposed metal joints of the frame.

"It's not slander, it's libel," the law professor called after her. "But it's *neither*. Because we were linked romantically…. It just wasn't a very successful linkage."

Dana fought the urge to glance over her shoulder. She'd learned everything she wished to know at Belding's office, and said everything that she'd intended to say, yet she couldn't help feeling that the encounter had played out entirely to his advantage.

ఌ

ANOTHER FORTY-EIGHT HOURS PASSED before she had any further word from Belding. That was long enough for two more uninspired treks down the Yellow Brick Road, during the second of which a lollypop-wielding Munchkin suffered an epileptic fit and the Tin Man tore a ligament in his ankle. Yet none of this deterred the producer, Hank Bratton, who sent word that he'd booked an additional performance—a site-specific charity benefit at the governor's mansion in Providence, for which the actors would be paid double. This was lobbying, not altruism. If all went well, Lowery & Bratton hoped to secure state funding for a new playhouse and concert venue in what had once been Creve Coeur's tenderloin district. The backers did not appear concerned that the show, on location, would have to run without set or lights.

"Of course he doesn't care," Docherty grumbled. "You know what he did before he started funding kids' musicals? He sold defoliant to Third World armies."

Dana glanced up from her magazine. It was Monday, a day of rest, and they were lounging in the Equity flophouse, waiting for the winged monkey to return from jogging so they could take a drive out to the public beach.

"You're making that up," she said.

"I'm dead serious. I read about it online. Which reminds me, have you checked out your Wikipedia tribute recently?"

She hadn't. She'd decided to put her encounter with Belding behind her. Docherty had called it right: if she ignored the lawyer, he'd likely leave her alone. Later, once his interest had waned, she could delete his unfounded claims from the Internet with impunity.

"I have to hand it to the bloke," Docherty said. "He's certainly persistent."

The Scotsman peered over his laptop at her, his rugged features alive with mischief. The dancer was like a tiny devil ensconced atop her shoulder, dangling his feet and kicking her periodically—and she knew it, too—yet still, she took his bait and let the Scotsman show her Belding's most recent handiwork:

Dana Whitlock (b. February 21, 1973, in Creve Coeur, Rhode Island) is an American character actress known for her great beauty, particularly her penetrating green eyes and ravishing smile. She is also noted for her versatility, including her ability to shift rapidly from hostility to affection.

Whitlock graduated from Roger Williams High School in Creve Coeur and attended the New York Stage and Film Academy. She is currently starring as Glinda, the Good Witch of the North, in a regional production of *The Wizard of Oz*. She lives in New York City.

RENDEZVOUS IN WIKITERNITY

Miss Whitlock has been romantically linked to attorney Caleb Belding. She initially met Belding during high school, and they rekindled their relationship after a chance meeting eighteen years later.

A link had been added to the generous review of *Oz* in *The Newport Daily News*.

"It's just brilliant," Docherty said. "What woman is going to delete a description of her own penetrating green eyes and ravishing smile?"

"Not me," Dana said. "You can scrap that last paragraph and leave the rest."

"Should I change the year of birth again, too?"

"Don't bother." She retrieved an unsweetened yogurt from the refrigerator and allowed the cool cream to melt over her tongue. "What's the point? I fear my moment of truth has finally arrived. So shout it from the rooftops! Let the world know that I'm old."

Maybe it was the discovery that Belding was not a complete stranger, or the flattering tone of his fabrications, but his embellishments no longer enraged her. Rather, they were more like the transgressions of a wayward child—to be corrected firmly, but without anger. So when she checked her biography on Docherty's laptop later that evening, she was actually amused to read Belding's latest contribution:

Dana Whitlock (b. February 21, 1973, in Creve Coeur, Rhode Island) is an American character actress known for her unequaled beauty, particularly her penetrating green eyes and ravishing smile. So great is her beauty that men have been known to stop in their tracks at the first glimpse of her flawless visage, dropping pianos mid-hoist and driving into unsuspecting trees.

The attorney had also restored the deleted paragraph at the end of the article and appended a second set of links to Dana's *Hedda Gabler* reviews. He'd included only the most favorable notices, principally from local Berkshire weeklies, ignoring the more equivocal verdicts in *The Boston Globe* and *Hartford Courant*. She didn't know whether she should feel alarmed or grateful for these attentions. More than anything else, she found herself confused.

Dana's biography—and her Wikipedia suitor—rapidly became the talk of the set. Miss Mass. and the one-time ingénue who played the cowardly lioness both thought the intrigue was creepy, even dangerous, and urged her to contact the authorities. But the square-jawed wardrobe mistress and Grayson Blank, a television veteran doomed to cap off his career as a regional wizard, thought they saw in Belding's efforts a romance fit for a medieval princess.

"Take it while you can get it, honey," urged the wardrobe mistress. "Lap it all up."

According to the winged monkey's Ouija board, which had recently predicted the "twist of fate" that had turned out to be the Tin Man's busted ankle, Dana's torrid romance lay as near as the cardboard turrets of the Emerald City. So she enjoyed the increasing effusiveness of Caleb Belding's ongoing Wikipedia homage, over the next few days, even as she dutifully reverted his edits. It was a late-night phone call from Jayson that finally shook her from her bewildered reverie.

"I was Googling myself this morning between shoots," said Jayson, who was filming a series of commercials for the Staten Island Ferry, "and then I remembered what you'd said about that Wikipedia thing, so I looked you up, too." A long, uneasy pause followed. "Tell it to me straight. What's going on between you and this guy Belding?"

"Jesus Christ, Jay. *Nothing.* Nothing is going on between me and Caleb Belding," she insisted, aware that she sounded far too defensive. "Absolutely nothing. If you ever listened to a word I said, you'd already know that."

"Okay, I believe you," her boyfriend replied, irking her by his implication that the possibility of not believing her had ever existed. "But, honestly, you've got to check out some of the shit that's written about you two. It sounds like you're practically married."

"I'll take care of it. I promise."

"Don't worry. I'm not jealous, baby," Jayson said. "Jealousy isn't my thing."

But she wanted a man who wasn't jealous because he trusted her—not because he was indifferent to her actions. With Jayson, she could never be sure. In contrast, she sensed that Caleb Belding would expect to know his partner's comings and goings, much as he would willingly share his own. If that was maturity, it struck Dana as somewhat terrifying.

The next morning, she logged onto Docherty's computer and enjoyed one final chapter of Belding's praise:

> Dana Whitlock (b. February 21, 1973, in Creve Coeur, Rhode Island) is an American character actress known for her unequaled beauty, particularly her penetrating green eyes and ravishing smile. So great is her beauty that Paris, seeing a sculpture of Whitlock, willingly returned Helen to the Greeks.

That was the sort of admiration a girl could get used to, and far more than she'd been receiving in the years since she'd turned thirty. But, deep down, she recognized that common sense favored the view of Miss. Mass. and the cowardly lioness. His scribblings should feel creepy. And no sane person ought to tolerate the detailed description of their "blissful" first date that Belding had included at the end of his latest revision—at Chez Raymond, the city's finest French restaurant, on an evening three nights into the future.

Dana replaced Wikipedia's lavish description of their romantic rendezvous with a single, unequivocal sentence:

> Miss Whitlock has denied any romantic involvement with Caleb Belding.

With Docherty's assistance, she then created a hypertext link that connected Caleb Belding's name to a Wikipedia page of his own. Here, she typed:

> Caleb G. Belding is a Rhode Island lawyer known for his zealous litigation. However, this determination often clouds his judgment. In one recent case, that of Miss Dana Whitlock, he failed to appreciate the depth of Miss Whitlock's attachment to her boyfriend, and made a pest of himself.

The Scotsman shook his head in obvious disappointment as he read what she'd written. "Are you sure you want to post this?"

"No, I'm not," Dana admitted. "But I'm doing it anyway."

When she checked the site a few hours later, during her forty-minute break between visits to Munchkinland and Oz, the lawyer had already altered his profile. It now read:

> Caleb G. Belding (b. November 27, 1974, in Westerly, Rhode Island) is an American attorney who specializes in copyright and trademark litigation. He is single and lives in Stonington, Connecticut.

Her own page remained as she'd left it. The excessive commentary on her beauty remained intact, but now it rang inexplicably sterile, like a tribute to the virtue of a long-departed saint.

Dana logged onto Wikipedia nearly every waking hour over the next five days, sometimes even multiple times during the same performance, secretly hoping, in spite of herself, that there might be further additions to either Belding's biography or hers. But it was not to be. The text of both entries remained provocatively unaltered.

☙

DANA HAD GONE COMPUTER-FREE for thirty-six hours, at Docherty's urging, when the moment arrived for their cast outing to the governor's mansion, and she determined not to examine her page "one last time" before the show. Instead, she passed the ride listening to Grayson Blank's tales of life in Creve Coeur during the Eisenhower years, when the city still supplied America's housewives with one hundred percent of their steel thimbles. In the rear of the bus, Vince Pepper did tarot readings for the director's children, high school girls who'd pressured their father into bringing along the entire family. Dana enjoyed herself. For the first time since the Scarecrow had discovered her Wikipedia page, she wasn't thinking about Caleb Belding.

The benefit itself proved a disaster. As a leading society columnist wrote the following morning in *The Providence Journal*, "This rendition of *Oz* brought 300 years of theatrical magic in New England to a grinding halt." The play was staged in the chief executive's ballroom, where the spectators sat on folding chairs, and a cleverly draped damask curtain served as a makeshift proscenium. Unfortunately, without the rotating stage that transformed Kansas into Oz, many of the Munchkins missed their entrance cues, and Auntie Em and Dana found themselves on stage simultaneously. Then one of the safety pins came loose on Dorothy's pinafore, giving the First Family an unexpected glimpse of Miss Mass.'s brassiere. And Toto, never one of the most obedient stage dogs in the business, took a liking to the governor's wife and detoured into the audience to be nuzzled. But the *piece de resistance*—the number that cut short the show—occurred when the Wicked Witch confronted Ian Docherty and the limping Tin Man in a wooded patch beside the Yellow Brick Road. At the theater in Creve Coeur, when the actress playing the witch demanded, "Do you want to play ball, Scarecrow?" she squeezed a button on her flame-proof glove that briefly activated a kerosene torch. The fiery effect was consistently one of the highlights of the show, guaranteed to awe hapless eight year olds. Yet at the governor's mansion, the witch miscalculated the distance between herself and the strawman, exposing him to errant sparks. In seconds, Docherty's costume ignited like flambé. The performance ended abruptly with the Scotsman rolling on the goldenrod carpet, while political staffers shrieked and the state police whisked the governor to safety.

Dana accompanied the injured dancer inside the ambulance. While his straw costume had burned intensely, making it appear as though his entire body had been engulfed in flames, the damage proved far less severe than the audience might have expected. Docherty had painful, third-degree burns on both shoulders and his left thigh, but the skin damage wasn't extensive enough to put his life or long-term health in jeopardy. Still, the medical team informed Dana, who one resident mistook for the Scotsman's wife, and another for his daughter, that the recovery could take months. Once he'd been settled into the intensive care unit, Docherty squeezed Dana's wrist and drifted into a morphine-induced haze. She retreated to the elevator bay and called her boyfriend on the payphone.

"How'd the show go?" Jayson asked.

"I'm at the hospital," she explained. "God, Jay, it was so awful. Ian caught on fire."

Saying the words made the tragedy real. And horrific. The telephone receiver trembled violently in her grip.

"Remind me," Jayson said. "Ian?"

"Ian Docherty," she answered, feeling the tears pool behind her eyes. "My friend who plays the Scarecrow."

"Oh, that's right. The Irish dude. "

At that moment, an elderly man exited the elevators carrying a vase of bearded irises. Dana watched him shuffle down the corridor and disappear.

"Yep, you've got it. The Irish dude."

"I'm sorry."

"Me, too."

When she hung up the phone, she bid goodnight to the

nonresponsive Docherty, kissing his forehead, then asked the night nurse if she might use one of the hospital computers. This violated official policy, Dana was informed, but the girl didn't give her a hard time.

"Just don't tell anyone, okay?" the nurse warned, then logged Dana onto the machine.

Her Wikipedia biography remained precisely as she left it. She erased the line:

> Miss Whitlock has denied any romantic involvement with Caleb Belding.

In its place, she typed:

> Miss Whitlock has reconsidered Caleb Belding's invitation and would be pleased to meet him for dinner at Chez Raymond.

Unable to sleep, she passed the next several hours creating additional Wikipedia biographies for the other members of the cast. She also added an entry for Hank Bratton, who had indeed, according to Google, made a fortune selling toxic weaponry in Southeast Asia. When she checked her own entry one final time, around five in the morning, before heading off to doze in the family lounge, she found that Belding had replaced her contribution with:

> Miss Whitlock and Mr. Belding will dine at Chez Raymond at 8 o'clock this evening.

☙

THE LAW PROFESSOR WAS ALREADY waiting for her at the crowded bar when she arrived. He sported a stylish Italian suit and—to her amazement—he'd even brought her a solitary red rose. With her permission, Belding snapped off the stem and tucked the blossom into her hair.

"I told them I was expecting the most beautiful woman in Rhode Island," he explained, "but at Chez Raymond, even perfection has to wait for a table."

He rose from his bar stool and chivalrously drew hers back, like a waiter at a fine restaurant. She hadn't realized how tall her date was before—over six feet. Her eyes rose to the same level as his shoulders.

"How's your friend?" he asked. "I recognized his photo in the paper."

"Surviving. He's lucky it happened on the job. Now Equity insurance covers him forever."

"And how are you? I thought I'd lost you again."

He gazed straight into her—with confidence—and she averted her eyes nervously, examining the wall of exotic beverages on the shelves behind the bar. The sounds of clattering dishes and angry Portuguese shouting drifted in from the nearby kitchen.

"I'm sorry I blew you off," she said.

"In twelfth grade? Or last week?"

"Both. But I actually meant in twelfth grade."

"You're forgiven," Belding said. "Just this once."

He smiled at her. She toyed with a cardboard coaster. The bartender refilled Belding's wineglass and brought Dana a snifter of cranberry juice.

"I do hope you realize how lucky you are—how lucky we are," he added. "I don't know if you've logged onto Wikipedia recently, but your entry has been deleted." Then he mimicked the message that had been posted on her page, serving up his rendition of a haughty English accent. *"It appears that, as per the consensus of our editors, Dana Whitlock does not meet the established standards of notability for living persons."*

"That's certainly a confidence booster," she said.

"At least we have one thing in common. I apparently don't meet their lofty standards, either."

"So we've *both* been deleted?"

Belding raised his glass. "To a non-notable couple." •

Long Term

"IRON LUNGS," CARL PITCHED. "A theme restaurant."

Phillip and his kid brother—if you could still be a kid brother at sixty-six—sat face-to-face in what had recently been Phillip's examination room. The cabinets stood open and bare, as though looted. Phillip had already locked his personal effects in the trunk of a colleague's car. All that remained in the oncologist's suite were a single wooden chair, a scale, a stainless-steel magazine stand, a removable wall clock, and two posters. One of the posters depicted foods high in fiber. The other was titled *What Every Man Should Know About Cancer of the Testicles.* It was the same throughout the hospital: ghostly wards, gurneys stacked in the nurses' stations. The desolate surroundings made Carl's pleas to his brother somehow more desperate.

"We'll have people dine inside the iron lungs," Carl said. "Or maybe on top of them. We can work out the details later."

"I take it that's a royal we," Phillip answered.

The words came out harsher than he'd intended. But it had all happened so fast—his tumor, the closing of the hospital, the iron-lung hullabaloo—that words had acquired new and surprising meanings. If he weren't dying, Phillip had quipped to his great-niece, he'd have written a Berlitz guide to cancer.

Carl looked down into his big hands. Phillip, on the rare occasions he was asked, described their relationship as "brotherly." The antithesis of intimate, a distance tinged with regret. Carl's prison stint hadn't helped any. One of his earlier restaurants, a Tex-Mex grill on Staten Island, had also served up laundered money. He'd done three years for conspiracy. Phillip's marriage had failed around the same time, and the two brothers struck up a correspondence. They exchanged frank, soul-bearing letters. These were the only personal letters Phillip ever wrote, so he lathered them with emotion, expressing what he'd never have thought to say. It had ended abruptly with Carl's parole. After that, they'd drifted.

Phillip circled aimlessly in his wheelchair, forcing his brother to twist his neck. He had already pledged the iron lungs to the hospital rabbi. For charity.

"Look," Carl said, "I know I haven't been the greatest brother. The greatest anything. But I need this, Phil. Please."

"I know you do."

"It's a bit nuts. I recognize that. But people fall for all sorts of wacko things. Hula hoops. And what's that Corn Castle people visit in Nebraska?"

"Corn Palace. It's in South Dakota."

"You know what I'm saying."

Carl sat with his elbows propped on the back of his chair. He removed his glasses and cleaned them with his handkerchief. His brother had reached the age, Phillip noticed, when you could no longer distinguish his eyelids from his brow.

"You've had all this media," said Carl, his voice suddenly enthusiastic. "It just might work."

Not in a million years, Phillip knew. Not for Carl. His brother took after their father, the Michelangelo of poor judgment and second-rate ideas. But whether the restaurant flopped wasn't the point.

"Let me think it over," Phillip said.

He followed Carl to the door. In the corridor, a janitor was waxing the floors. His blower spun and bellowed. Hadn't they told him?

Phillip recalled an argument with his ex-wife. About why the musicians on the Titanic continued playing. Sharon thought them heroic. Phillip suspected they didn't know what else to do.

∽

TWO WEEKS AFTER THE HOSPITAL CLOSED, the iron lungs were delivered. The men from the shipping company—three bare-chested Israeli teenagers—set the capsules down on Phillip's front lawn in near-perfect rows. It was a sticky spring morning, and the oncologist rolled his wheelchair under the lindens to watch their efforts. He would have chosen the same patch of shade, most likely, even without the delivery. While his marriage had lasted, he'd never understood Sharon's passion for gardening. Her labor always seemed a no-win proposition, part of an endless cycle of blooming and wilting. Now he savored the syrupy aroma of peonies and lilacs. The shippers displayed no interest in the foliage. One by one, they hoisted the venerable machines off the truck. Mostly post-war Emerson models, but also duplex respirators from the 1930s. The straight rows reminded Phillip of the graves at military cemeteries.

One of the Israelis approached Phillip with a clipboard. He was a bulky young man with long black hair and a scar above his left eye. Handsome in a rugged way. His sweat-drenched T-shirt dangled from the belt loop of his shorts.

"All I need is your autograph, my friend," the deliveryman said.

Phillip braced the clipboard against the arm of the wheelchair. This signature business never made much sense to him. What stopped him from signing Ethel Barrymore? Or Joan of Arc? Nobody ever checked. Nonetheless, he did his best to pen Phillip C. Chapman, MD, in the narrow space allotted. Then he peeled three tens from his billfold. "For all of you," he said.

"Thank you, my friend."

It struck Phillip that the shippers might not be Israeli at all—that the language he'd taken for Hebrew might be Arabic.

"May I ask you a question?" asked the youth.

Phillip looked up, without speaking.

The youth grinned broadly. "Did you work with the space program?"

"Me?" answered Phillip, surprised. "I'm a physician." He'd expected the young man to ask him about his illness, or possibly the iron lungs. A moment later, he realized that the young man was asking about the iron lungs. How easy to mistake them for vessels of the early NASA fleet.

"They're iron lungs," explained Phillip. "For polio."

"Interesting," said the youth. His tone suggested disappointment.

"People used to live in them," Phillip added.

The youth smiled and stepped backward. "Thanks again, doc," he said, holding up the thirty dollars, then inching beyond the range of conversation.

Soon Phillip was alone. His great-niece, Katrina, had gone off to her quilting class. It was already too late for joggers, too early for the mail. Another hour would pass before half-day dismissal at the kindergarten. How strange this languorous suburban stillness! Never before had Phillip contemplated different varieties of stillness, but there was no mistaking this torpor for the eerie calm of the vacated hospital. He wanted to share this minor revelation—but who was available to chat during the workday? His colleagues now worked at other hospitals, after all. Getting on with their lives.

Once a despondent patient had said to Phillip: "I don't want to live my life over again. I just want to take it back—to leave a neutral, a blank slate. Like Jimmy Stewart in *It's a Wonderful Life*." Phillip had never wished for either. Sixty-eight good years were far preferable to many more bad ones. He'd walked on six continents. He'd slept with beautiful women. His lymphoma studies had saved countless lives. Not even the toxic cells in his gray matter could take that away from him. Maybe that's what made it possible to forgo the useless chemotherapy, to ignore his friends' pleas of Doctor, heal thyself! Not easy, but possible. Likewise, the decision to shut the hospital hadn't fazed him. He accepted the verdict of the marketplace, the steel laws of supply and demand. Yet now, for the first time in months, he grew angry. This iron-lung fiasco was too much—one last kick from the boot of fate. Why should the decision fall on his shoulders? Phillip wasn't religious. His believed in a Jeffersonian deity, a cosmic watchmaker. Yet the lung brouhaha felt like a final examination in mortality.

℃℈

FOR DECADES, NOBODY ELSE had taken an interest in the iron lungs. They'd been packed head-to-toe in the basement of the Women's & Infants' Pavilion. The same alcove—a cluttered, cedar-paneled vestibule behind the boiler room—also contained cobwebbed caterers' carts and the vinyl chairs from the old hospital barbershop. Detritus. Junk. At one time, tours of prospective medical students paraded through the space to see the historic collection. In recent years, the guides merely spoke of its existence. Iron lungs, wooden legs, glass eyes, they said. Weird shit. None of the new guides, of course, had actually seen the capsules. Occasionally, Phillip found evidence of human exploration in the basement: hamburger wrappers, a woman's stocking. But some years—it was rare that the oncologist made more than one annual pilgrimage to the cellar—dust coated the floorboards like virgin snow.

Phillip had come to Morningside General in 1957. That was the same year Leonard Hawkins's *The Man in the Iron Lung* topped the bestseller list, but already the airtight pods were losing ground to history. Bird-Mark respirators had entered the marketplace. Salk's vaccine was stamping out bulbar polio. The two-thousand-dollar machines, once recirculated within hours of a patient's death, sometimes stood idle for months. Eventually, in the early sixties, the chief of pulmonary decided to toss the lot of them. His name was Leveret, Phillip recalled. A crusty New Englander. (Shortly afterward, he burst an aneurysm in his chest.) When Phillip requested the iron lungs, the pulmonologist shook his head and called him a sentimentalist. Ungodly coffins, he added. Good riddance to bad rubbish. Leveret sold the machines to Phillip for one dollar each. He never asked his junior colleague what he intended to do with them. Which was good, because Phillip hadn't known. And still didn't know. If he'd owned Lionel trains or stuffed animals as a child, he'd have kept those, too.

❧

PHILLIP'S MOTHER HAD DIED OF CANCER. When Katrina asked about the iron lungs, that seemed the logical place to start. The girl was his great-niece. Joan's granddaughter, rest his sister's soul. Katrina had graduated from Bryn Mawr the previous spring with a degree in folklore studies, but wasn't sure what came next. In the interim, she looked after her fading uncle. Buying his groceries. Watering his daylilies. Changing the sheets on his deathbed. It was free room and board—better than her parents' place in California. Weekends, she waitressed at Waterford's Tavern. She was a real head-turner: deep black eyes, high breasts, a waterfall of cocoa hair. The men who took her out all vaguely resembled Tab Hunter, only shaggier. Often, she didn't come home at night. It entered Phillip's imagination that she might fall in love with him— although he knew this was laughable. A thought to be banished. Yet he sensed an added spark inside himself whenever she joined him on the patio to hear his stories.

"What kind of cancer?" Katrina asked. She wanted to know everything, the whole story—the opposite of the reporters from *The Daily Clarion*. Natural curiosity, maybe. Or a desire to milk him dry before his passing.

"Maybe an adenocarcinoma of the esophagus," Phillip said. "At least, that's consistent with what I remember. It could have spread to her lungs and spine."

All speculation, obviously. Like these "investigative pathologists" who tried to prove that Charlemagne had been poisoned or Eleanor Roosevelt had died of undiagnosed tuberculosis. So much bunk. Phillip's father, a small-town stationer, had always called it cancer. Nothing more. Nothing less. (If "Ace" Chapman had known anything else, and Phillip doubted so very much, it was another scrap of knowledge lost to oblivion.) Among the three of them—Joan, Carl, and himself—they hadn't even remembered the names of their mother's doctors. Not that it mattered. Who saved medical records from 1945?

"You don't know?" Katrina persisted.

"We lived in a different world. Mama didn't even know she had cancer. None of us did. It was a secret between our father and the doctors."

Katrina whistled. "Wow."

"They told her it was an ulcer, a herniated disk."

"That's awful."

"They still do that some places," Phillip said. "The Middle East, parts of Japan."

She refilled his lemonade glass, then her own. "Maybe I should be tape-recording this."

"Maybe."

"It's almost too much to process."

What Phillip wanted to answer was: "And that's not the half of it." He hadn't told her about her grandmother's elopement—his sister's first marriage—with that walleyed Italian pharmacist. The couple had met at Brückner's Drugs when Joan went to purchase castor oil for their mother's "chronic indigestion." Three weeks later, while Doris Chapman's organs collapsed like dominoes, her oblivious nineteen-year-old daughter was exchanging vows at a Catholic church in Camden,

New Jersey. And worse yet: that poor pharmacist spent his honeymoon sitting shivah on a wooden crate, his bride's uncles sizing him up like rancid meat. For thirty years in America, they'd spoken English. Only English. But those seven days, they spoke Yiddish. Extending themselves to make the groom uncomfortable. Once the pharmacist departed—three weeks later—Joan never uttered his name again. Phillip saw no need to do so now.

"How did you find out?" Katrina asked.

It was unclear whether she was referring to his mother's cancer or her death.

"A kid on the street told me. Chuck Sandow." Phillip paused and watched a black squirrel nibbling at the bird feeder.

Katrina nodded sympathetically: a perfect bedside manner.

"Your Uncle Carl and I had gone to spend the weekend with a boy in the next town over. Albert Katz. Or Alvin. He collected stamps, like your uncle. We ended up getting into a fight with the boy—Lord knows about what—so we decided to hike all the way home. On the corner of Grove Street and Palmer Avenue, Chuck Sandow comes up to us carrying a basketball and says, 'Your Ma's died.'"

Katrina cradled her tall lemonade glass in both hands. She appeared to be searching for the right words, but all she said was, "Wow."

"I still remember the basketball."

The sun dipped behind a cloudbank. Phillip sensed a chill run up his right arm. He no longer felt much of anything in his left arm.

"What did you do?" Katrina asked.

"Nothing. Not then," Phillip said. On the silver screen, he'd have pummeled Chuck Sandow—cut off his wind until the boy took it back. But East Putney wasn't Hollywood, and Chuck Sandow was too dopey to lie. All Phillip did was walk away without saying a word. "Later, we did stuff. Screwy stuff. Stealing road signs, slashing tires. One night, we coated the first-floor windows of the elementary school in black paint. Another time, we followed the paperboy around the neighborhood, undoing his work. I can't give you an explanation. Not a good one. But it made sense."

"You were angry."

"I suppose so," Phillip said. He didn't remember feeling angry, only dazed. As though the world were a massive hoax. "Your Uncle Carl was the brains of the operation. He finally did us in by ordering Frigidaires C.O.D. for the teachers we didn't like."

Katrina laughed richly, swirling the ice in her drink. "Fucking brilliant."

"That's how I ended up in the iron-lung ward. Community service. Nine months of weekends."

How long nine months had once seemed! He'd almost forgotten those odd divisions of the young person's calendar. Grades. Semesters. Medical clerkships. Katrina was "taking a year off." That made their time together extraneous.

The girl sat perched on the chaise longue, her bare legs crossed. She'd tucked her hair under a red bandana. "What was she like?" Katrina asked. "Your mother."

Doris Chapman (nee Kleinberg): a swimmer, a bridge player. People said she'd loved dancing and ice skating, though Phillip could never recall her doing either. He did remember warnings not to walk under ladders or place new shoes on tables. Carl had been her favorite, her baby.

"What was Mama like?" Phillip said. "I sometimes wonder that myself."

∽

THE HOSPITAL WHERE PHILLIP performed his community service contained two iron-lung wards that shared a common solarium. One of these wards housed acute cases, polio victims for whom recovery still looked possible. After two or three months, the unluckiest patients were wheeled down the corridor to the long-term unit. This was a whitewashed rectangular chamber with tremendously high ceilings. It reminded Phillip of a hospital scene in a movie about the Crimean War. The room's lethargic fans proved no match for the summer heat or the fusty smell of institutional living. Patients lay aligned in dormitory ranks, confined neck-to-toe in pressurized shells. These were all men—it was an all-male unit—with no place else to go.

Phillip's job was to operate the movie projector on Saturday afternoons. Those were visiting hours, but few "lifers" received visitors. Sundays were less structured. He ran errands for the nurses, read aloud. A ward mascot. Carl was assigned to polish flatware in the physicians' dining room; it had been thought wise to separate them.

Patients knew one pleasure. Talking. Phillip learned to listen to their stories.

Kenny Trundle hadn't had polio. He was a municipal engineer who'd fallen off the roof of a streetcar, a fact that he shared with anyone and everyone, maybe believing it elevated him above his companions.

Jim van Pelt rooted religiously for the St. Louis Browns. The other patients called him "Slugger," because he sincerely believed he would play baseball again. "They've come up with sulfa drugs, antibiotics," he insisted. "We're next."

Cass Kaye, a Southerner in his early thirties, had the strongest impact on Phillip. He'd been married, but his wife had died. Septicemia. He'd also had a sister bitten by a rabid dog. Kaye coped by honing his anger against the late President Roosevelt. For us, ranted Kaye, he did nothing. Nothing. "Us" meant other polio victims, men who couldn't hide behind pince-nez and stylish cigarette holders. Guys who can't reach our own pricks! This was a plea, of course. Disguised. Unanswered. (Years later, Phillip regretted his own selfishness.) One afternoon, Kaye broke. He bit a finger off the shift nurse and was transferred elsewhere.

Phillip found himself staggered by the sheer scope and enormity of human misfortune. His own suffering had seemed an island. At the hospital, he recognized it as belonging to an archipelago of misery. Like the patients, he escaped into the movies. Bergman & Crosby in *The Bell's of St. Mary's*. Hitchcock's *Spellbound*. *The Lost Weekend* with Ray Milland. Many of the films were recycled annually. Phillip had no idea who chose them, or why.

They screened *Dark Victory* in October: Bette Davis starred as the heiress whose surgeon husband doesn't tell her she's dying. George Brent played the husband. In the final scene, Davis discovers the secret—and dies anyway.

⅌

THE FINANCIAL VALUE of the iron lungs had never occurred to Phillip. In the first place, he had no instinct for—or much interest in—money. When Sharon left, he'd let her take almost everything. The house. The timeshare on Cormorant Island. Half of his future pension. It didn't matter to him that her new fiancé, a high-end motivational speaker, drove an Aston Martin convertible. Phillip also possessed an instinctive aversion to get-rich-quick schemes, something for nothing. That had been his father's strong suit. Ace Chapman nearly bankrupted himself printing "novelty" greeting cards: "It Was About Time You Broke The Engagement," "Congratulations on Your Workers' Comp Claim." Later, he sank his savings into laetrile, otter farming, bauxite mines in the Far East. So when Phillip heard of the miracles of the Internet—$17,000 for Greta Garbo's dog license, twice that for a strand of Lindbergh's hair—he didn't connect them to his own life. His concerns were biopsy results, platelet counts.

Soon after the hospital board's fatal announcement, Rabbi Binder surprised Phillip with a visit to his office. The rabbi was a stout man with short arms. Modern in outlook, traditional in practice, droll. At a panel discussion on "Cancer & Prayer," Phillip had once heard him enumerate the three Jewish viewpoints regarding euthanasia: "No," "No," and

"No." He made Phillip less uneasy than other rabbis.

"Make yourself at home, Rabbi," Phillip said. He considered asking, "How's God doing these days?" But didn't.

"Sorry to drop in unannounced," Binder said. "I'll take only a moment."

The rabbi sat down and the swivel chair creaked beneath his weight. He cupped his hands together against his abdomen, palms up, like a pouch.

"I'm not so busy," Phillip answered. "I've been tapering my practice."

"So I've heard. You have my thoughts and my prayers."

"What I really need is a good chauffeur."

Binder smiled through his beard. Phillip toyed with a jade paperweight from his desk, rolling the cylinder along the blotter. In the first days after his diagnosis, he'd actually contemplated speaking to the rabbi. He was now thankful that he hadn't. It surprised him how little they had to say to each other.

"In any case," Binder said, "I've come hat in hand."

So this was it, Phillip thought. He'd always counted Binder above that.

"There's a third-year medical student doing a supplemental degree in divinity," Binder continued. "She tells me you have some sort of museum in the basement."

"Old equipment. All out of date."

It struck the oncologist for the first time that with the hospital shuttering its doors, he'd have to move the iron lungs. Or discard them. Izzy Kaplan, when he'd been chief of medicine, had permitted Phillip to store the capsules in the cellar. After Kaplan died, inertia had kept them in place.

"This girl says you have iron lungs down there. Dozens of them."

"Sixty-one," Phillip answered.

That was when the rabbi hit him up for the donation. According to Binder, the collectibles establishment was lung-happy. His machines could fetch up to three thousand dollars. (The man had done his homework.)

"What does that come to?" Phillip asked. "Fifty dollars a lung?"

The rabbi leaned forward. "I'm afraid you've misunderstood me. That's up to three thousand *each*."

"Each," Phillip repeated.

"Enough to feed hundreds of families," Binder added. "A mitzvah. A worthy legacy. Unless you object, that is."

Phillip was still doing the math in his head. "I don't see why I would," he said.

The rabbi chuckled. "You drive a hard bargain."

They had concluded the meeting with a handshake. (It was strange to shake hands when you no longer had sensation in your fingers.) But what was the significance of a handshake? Ethically? Legally? Might it be pre-empted by other needs?

The Daily Clarion phoned the following morning. They ran the iron-lung story as a human-interest feature on Page 1.

In the story, Phillip expressed only his intention to give away the machines. He avoided specifics. (Who knew whether Binder wanted publicity?) That's how Carl had learned of the iron lungs—along with every other civic organization, church mission, artists' collective, animal shelter, and brazen swindler in the county. *The Clarion* also supplied a price estimate: $150,000.

Television picked up the story. There was no choice but to un-jack the phones.

"For all the anxiety they've caused," he told Katrina, "I should bury myself with them. Like the ancient Egyptians."

"Or I could eat them," he added later. "Piece by piece."

ↈ

DURING HIS FINAL DAYS at the hospital, Phillip took pains to avoid the rabbi. He also stayed clear of his office suite—afraid Carl might find him. It was like those radio advertisements for loan consolidation: Are creditors hounding you? Are you afraid to open your front door? Yet one could buy only so much time. (And time was Phillip's most precious possession. Soon he'd be aphasiac, consigned to spelling simple words with children's wooden blocks. Or stiff as a petrified log. The progress of the disease varied from patient to patient. There was no helping that. At least not in a way that sat well with Phillip's conscience. All of his other affairs were in order. He'd left letters for his great-niece and one of his colleagues, a pediatrician he'd considered dating, but hadn't. What money remained, and there wasn't much, would pay medical bills. Once he'd disbursed the iron lungs, he could die a "good" death.) Now the capsules blanketed Phillip's lawn, taunting him.

Binder might call this a warning: a righteous, Old Testament God admonishing him for accepting death too easily, for growing vain in his own acquiescence. To Phillip, this was so much hooey. He saw it as merely a clash of obligations. Not a choice between his brother and humanity, but a choice between isotopes of guilt.

Katrina's car pulled into the driveway. It had once been Phillip's car. An Oldsmobile—classy, yet never top-of-the-line.

Phillip was still sitting under the lindens. He watched his great-niece unloading groceries from the vehicle, placing the bags on the hood. She came up the path with one bag braced on each hip, her quilting satchel hanging off her shoulder. The girl's denim skirt didn't reach her knees.

"Jesus fucking Christ," Katrina exclaimed. "What's all this junk?"

Such a strange creature the girl was. It was difficult to reconcile quilting and folklore with all that profanity.

"I told you the lungs were arriving today," Phillip said.

"Oh, of course." She adjusted her hold on the bags. "I guess I expected something smaller. More lung-like."

Phillip found this endearing.

"How was class?" he asked.

She winced—overdramatically. "The professor's going to make a pass at me."

"Are you sure?"

"He hasn't yet, but it's coming. I can tell."

Phillip waited for her to add: "He's your age." But she didn't.

Katrina laughed without warning. She did that sometimes. When Phillip asked what was funny, she just shrugged. "Did you figure out what you're going to do with the lungs?"

"I thought I'd leave them on the lawn as an art installation," said Phillip. "It'll work wonders for property values."

The girl had suggested dividing the capsules in half. Like Solomon and the baby. But Solomon didn't have Carl Chapman for a brother. Phillip already knew what Carl's response would be.

"Half isn't enough. Not for a theme restaurant." Once he'd said that, it didn't matter to either of them whether it was true.

Katrina's cellphone rang. Or, rather, it played a tune Phillip didn't recognize. His great-niece gently set the grocery bags onto the grass. "Hello?"

"For you," she said, extending the phone. "Uncle Carl."

Phillip had no choice. He took hold of the tiny device. Katrina mouthed the word "perishables" and pointed at the grocery bags, then disappeared into the house.

"I finally found you! Your answering machine isn't working," Carl said. "I was getting ready to call out the bloodhounds."

"I don't think any bloodhounds will be necessary."

Phillip held the receiver some distance from his ear. He wasn't particularly fond of cellphones—or most consumer gadgetry, for that matter. "A misappropriation of resources," he'd informed Katrina. "Any enlightened society would spend the money on medical research." Also, the devices made him nervous.

"Do you know where I am?" Carl asked.

"How could I possibly know where you are?"

"I'm at a payphone. On River Street in Clark Valley. Across from the train station."

Clark Valley was two towns over. No place special.

"Okay," Phillip said.

"I've found the most perfect storefront," he said. "You know how it is: location, location, location. The rent's a bit pricey, but I'll talk them down."

Carl spoke rapidly. He sounded like an extremely nervous man struggling to feign confidence.

"We've got backers now," he continued. "They saw that piece on Channel 3 and fell in love with the idea."

"I didn't promise anything," Phillip said. "I said I'd let you know."

Carl said nothing. Phillip heard traffic in the distance. He could picture his brother at the phone booth—sparse hair heavily gelled, shirt rumpled despite his best efforts. Far removed from the spiffy teenage truant who'd once coated neighbors' doorknobs in Vaseline. At thirty-five, Carl had looked very much the rising entrepreneur. Now, he appeared as though he'd been pensioned by a limousine service. Yet Carl was his kid brother, his best friend until the age of thirteen.

"I don't know," Phillip said.

"I've got to have this. I won't have another chance."

Katrina crossed the yard to retrieve more groceries. Phillip watched her passing between the ranks of lifeless capsules. All of the men who'd occupied them—men like "Slugger" van Pelt and Cass Kaye—were long dead. How would they feel about having suburban children slurping pasta off their one-time prisons? Would they find it degrading? Humorous? Would they care at all?

Phillip turned his head skyward. A raindrop.

"Look, Carl," he said. "I can't do it. I'm sorry." He didn't know where the words came from. They just happened.

Silence. Another raindrop: the makings of a sun shower.

"All right," said Carl, more to himself than Phillip. "I can handle that."

More silence. "All right," Carl repeated.

"I have to go now," Phillip said. "It's starting to rain."

Carl ignored him. "Who are you going to give them to?" His voice rose. "Who's more important than YOUR OWN GODDAMN BROTHER?"

"It's not about more important. But really, I have to go. I'll call you back in a few minutes. I swear."

He poked at the buttons on the phone, more or less randomly, trying to shut off the device before Carl said anything else. After several tries, the line went dead.

"Katrina!" he shouted. "Katrina!"

She wasn't in the yard. She wasn't in the driveway. The raindrops intensified. A few more minutes and the shower would soak the capsules. It was like watching fire nibble through a precious document.

"Katrina! Where the hell are you?"

The girl appeared from the direction he least expected. Around the side of the house. Behind her trailed a tangled blue tarp.

"It's all I could find," she said. "It should cover most of them."

Phillip watched his great-niece work. The tarp was a remnant of his married life, from before he'd had the swimming pool permanently drained. Sharon had been a swimmer. Like his mother. He'd considered filling it again—for Katrina. But she preferred to do her laps at a local college gym. The girl worked out every morning before breakfast, and it showed. *Mens sana in corpore sano.* Some young man was going to be extremely fortunate.

Katrina managed to cover all but two iron lungs. She tried to lug the outliers under the canvas, but couldn't.

"It's not worth it," said Phillip.

His great-niece stood hands on her hips, short of breath, her wet skin glistening. "That's five thousand dollars," she said.

"The love of money is the root of all evil."

"Easy to say," Katrina said, "if you've got it."

She had a point. She always had a point. "What would you do with sixty-one iron lungs?" Phillip asked.

The girl raked her fingertips through her hair. "I'd sell them," she said. "I'd go back to school."

Not the answer Phillip had wanted. He realized—after asking the question—that he'd wanted her to say something about a museum. A shrine. His own dream would be to build a Louvre of iron lungs.

"Back to school for what?"

Katrina laughed. That enchanting laugh. "That's the other problem," she said. "I don't know yet." Her expression turned abruptly serious, intense. "I don't like to think about that. It stresses me out."

Phillip wondered if he'd ever seen another sight so captivating as his great-niece, at that moment, her hair shimmering with raindrops. He was sure he had, but it was no longer within emotional reach. The shower had stopped. Warm sunlight reflected off the puddles on the tarp. Katrina shivered slightly. She crossed her arms over her chest and stared thoughtfully into nowhere. Phillip was seized with a sudden desire to help her—not for her sake, but for his own. It was like buying her a romantic gift, flowers, lingerie, though nobody, including the girl, would ever see it that way.

"You'll put the money in the bank," he said, "until you figure it out."

ɕ

THEY ARRANGED THE PAPERWORK that afternoon. Phillip also wrote an apologetic letter to Rabbi Binder. Then he relaxed on the patio, alone, while the girl telephoned her parents in California. The day had turned mild. Orioles flitted through the apple blossoms. Several chipmunks cavorted on a nearby stone wall.

It amazed Phillip how well his life had turned out. Others might not see it that way, but he did. Of the world's vast and merciless suffering, he had experienced far less than his fair share. He had devoted many years to talking patients into surgery, radiation, chemotherapy. But medicine fixed bodies, not lives. His own life, for all its ordeals, had never been broken.

Phillip watched his great-niece through the glass doors of the patio. Glowing. Her lips moving a mile a minute. His thoughts drifted to his own college days, to his era of decision-making. He had screened movies in the long-term ward for another nine years, as a volunteer, watching Bette Davis in *Dark Victory* every October, agonizing between a career in medicine and in film.

Options had seemed a burden then, not a blessing. •

The Author

JACOB M. APPEL is a physician, attorney, and bioethicist based in New York City. Author of more than two hundred published short stories, he is a past winner of the *Boston Review* Short Fiction Competition, the William Faulkner-William Wisdom Award for the Short Story, the Dana Award, the Arts & Letters Prize for Fiction, *North American Review*'s Kurt Vonnegut Prize, *Missouri Review*'s Editor's Prize, *Sycamore Review*'s Wabash Prize, *Briar Cliff Review*'s Short Fiction Prize, the H. E. Francis Prize, the New Millennium Writings Fiction Award, an Elizabeth George Fellowship, and a Sherwood Anderson Foundation Writers Grant. His stories have been short-listed for the O. Henry Award, *Best American Short Stories*, *Best American Nonrequired Reading*, and the Pushcart Prize on numerous occasions. His nonfiction has appeared in *The New York Times*, *New York Post*, *New York Daily News*, *Chicago Tribune*, *San Francisco Chronicle*, and many other regional newspapers. Jacob holds graduate degrees from Brown University, Columbia University's College of Physicians and Surgeons, Harvard Law School, New York University's MFA program in fiction, and Albany Medical College's Alden March Institute of Bioethics. He taught for many years at Brown University, and currently teaches at the Gotham Writers' Workshop and the Mount Sinai School of Medicine.

Howling Bird Press

As part of the publishing concentration in the low-residency MFA in Creative Writing program at Augsburg College, Howling Bird Press serves to provide students with hands-on experience in the book trade. HBP sponsors an annual nationwide writing contest in which they select, edit, design, and publish the winning book— in this year's case, *The Topless Widow of Herkimer Street*, by Jacob M. Appel. Howling Bird wishes to acknowledge the efforts of associate editors Katherine Berger, Patricia Fox, and Cynthia Truitt Lynch, as well as MFA faculty and staff. Special thanks to supporters of the Howling Bird Press Publishing Fund, who—through Augsburg's Give to the Max campaign—provided generous support for this year's project: Louis Branca, Cass Dalglish, Ronald Blankenship, Susan Lucks, Kay Malchow, Dawn Matuseski, and Dr. Paul Pribbenow, along with many other donors. And gratitude to 2016 HBP fiction readers: Laurie Anderson, Katherine Berger, Stephan Clark, Cass Dalglish, Faith Ericson, Joshua Johnson, Mary Lewis, Sierra Miller, Jodi Napiorkowski, Gala Oliver, and Roseroberta Bobbi Pauling.